# DEADLY DIAGNOSIS

MAIRI CHONG

Copyright © 2020 by Mairi Chong

All rights reserved.

No part of this book may be reproduced in any form or by any electronic or mechanical means, including information storage and retrieval systems, without written permission from the author, except for the use of brief quotations in a book review.

All the characters in this book are fictitious, and any resemblance to actual persons living or dead, is purely coincidental.

IBSN: 978-1-913463-02-1 (print edition)

IBSN: 978-1-913463-03-8 (ebook edition)

*For W - forever and forever*

# 1

The man glided evenly across the polished floor, his white coat offering no resistance. Hands beneath his armpits dragged him slowly, purposefully.

A metallic click sounded, like the cock of a pistol, as the door behind them shut. He stirred, but his assailant was now busy by the wall. Although he did not know it, he was in the centre of the room. A window in the ceiling offered only bruised moonlight and even this was not much. The skylight itself was distorted with cobwebs and many years of grime.

He was barely conscious. Some awareness allowed him to shuffle his legs. He attempted to manoeuvre his limbs into position so that he might try to sit up. His arms were heavy, like sodden cloth. Useless. His fingers clawed and scratched at the linoleum. Exhausted, he lay back once more, panting. His breath came in heaves. Summoning his energy, he tried to speak. His dry lips twitched. He heard a mumbling noise that he didn't recognise, and then a snort. His assailant came across and stood above him. The man tried to look up, but his head would only lift as far as his attacker's ankles. His vision was blurred. He blinked uncomprehendingly. His mouth moved again, but this time, no noise came. The feet retreated once more.

A shiver ran through him. The movement made his body ache. His head pounded. It was easier with his eyes closed. The effort to open them again was too great anyway.

A hissing sound came from across the room. He had heard the sound before but could not place it. His eyelids fluttered and he forced them apart. Frowning hurt. His face relaxed into hopeless passivity once more.

Hands were now on his head. He wanted to pull away but couldn't. He managed to grunt, but the hands were relentless. Something sticky was placed on his temples. He tried to think. Stupid. Then came a moment of recollection. A blinding flash of realisation. He wished he had not remembered.

As the footsteps moved to the door, the hiss continued. He inhaled cool air for the last time. Thankfully, he did not hear the flick of the switch, nor was he aware of the sudden flame that engulfed the room after his attacker had closed the door.

His body lay shuddering and convulsing long into the night. Finally, the flames burnt through the wires to his forehead and allowed his charred remains to rest.

## 2

For a woman in her mid-thirties, Dr Cathy Moreland looked, if anything, far younger than her years. Her hair, recently cut, was glossy but, still not used to the length, she found herself tucking the ends behind her ear in a distracted manner. The thick jumper that she wore seemed to engulf her small frame, but it was necessary given the time of year.

The radiator by the window clunked twice. Cathy, without looking, stretched out her left leg and tapped the side of it with the heel of her shoe. It silenced almost immediately. She smiled and looking up from her notes, glanced sideways out of the window. Her last patient had been complicated and often, even when a person left her room, she found herself considering them and hoping that she had done the right thing. She would mentally carry their problems home with her at night often, and lie awake, wondering. She leant back in her chair and rubbed her forehead, as was her habit.

Before her illness, she had been more blasé. She had always followed up her consultations with the caveat that they should return if their symptoms worsened. This, she documented in the notes. As far as insurance purposes were concerned, she was covered. But these days, she regularly thought about the diagnoses she might have missed back in the early days. The patients whose lives, through her nonchalance, even conceit, might have suffered. But it was impossible to think like that. You could only do your utmost to help people at the time, and then let it go. Everyone in the profession knew that.

Her reflection in the window, cut at regular intervals by the hanging blinds, looked back, gaunt and weary. It had been a long week.

Outside, the street lights had already come on. It was only four o'clock but the sky had darkened and the rainclouds that had been gathering all late-afternoon were ready to release their offering. The patients who had been in to see her that day had said it was going to snow come the weekend, but so far, the menacing clouds had only given rise to a cold, damp drizzle.

Cathy sighed. She had a full surgery of patients to attend to that afternoon. She turned back from the window and looked once more at her computer screen. The receptionists had just added a message for her attention. She quickly scanned the contents. It wasn't unusual to have late requests for appointments on a Friday afternoon. Usually, however, the girls would field them, and if necessary, punt them in the direction of the duty doctor. That afternoon, Linda was on-call. As far as she knew, her colleague had had a fairly quiet day of it, with only a couple of emergency visits. Cathy couldn't understand why it wasn't Linda who had been sent the appointment request instead of herself. She re-read the message and typed a quick reply: *'Explain that I'm chock-a-block. If urgent, ask Linda. If not, book for next week.'*

She rose from her chair, seeing on the screen that her next patient was in. The man hadn't been in since his daughter had died the previous year and she wondered what he might have come for. She walked to the door of her consulting room and opened it, ready to call his name.

'Oh, I'm sorry,' she said, coming face-to-face with an elderly lady in the corridor right outside. 'Whose room are you looking for?'

The white-haired lady smiled. 'It's your room I'm after, Dr Moreland. I'm from the charity shop in town. A fundraiser, that was what it was. The girls at the desk said I couldn't get an appointment until next Thursday and they wouldn't listen when I told them it was only a quick word.'

Cathy smiled. 'They were right. I'm afraid I have a full surgery this afternoon. I'm very sorry, Mrs …'

'Oh, you don't know my name, it's Scott. Elizabeth Scott. I've not been in to see you before, but I had heard about your interest in …'

'I'm so sorry Mrs Scott. If you just come to the front desk with me, we'll sort out an appointment.'

She guided the woman back through the waiting area, ignoring her protestations that it would only take a couple of minutes, five at the most.

'Michelle,' Cathy said, coming to the desk and giving her receptionist a stern look. 'Next week, please. And find out what on earth Linda's doing.'

The tone of irritation was impossible to miss and the elderly lady, still fussing and remonstrating, was finally silenced. Cathy moved back through the waiting room. She called her next legitimate patient's name and stood by her door waiting. The girls were meant to be gate-keepers to the GPs. Michelle should have dealt with the whole situation far better. Cathy was breaking her back trying to field calls and requests. It was hardly fair to start allowing members of the public access to her at all hours of the day, and without even an appointment. And what was Linda doing anyway? She had no one booked-in, couldn't she have seen the old woman if it was that urgent?

Sitting down and trying to compose herself, Cathy sighed. 'Mr Stonley, it's been a while since we last saw you. What can I do for you today?'

∼

BARELY A WEEK LATER, Cathy looked at the patient before her and tried to gauge how much she knew. She was halfway through her morning surgery and had, up until then, seen a fairly predictable list.

'Oh, I know of course,' the woman said in answer to the unvoiced question. Her face, creased and Cathy was reminded of an old novel. The elderly lady's pallor was almost the same as the pages of one. The woman's eyes had an odd expression of almost pity, which was strange given the fact that she was the one dying. Elizabeth Scott was lying on Cathy's examination couch. She had pulled the curtain around for modesty and had been somewhat shocked by what her patient had initially described as 'a little matter.'

Cathy nodded. 'Why did you leave it?' she asked, withdrawing her hands.

The old woman pulled her blouse across her bare flesh again, screening the firm, irregular outline to her left breast. She shrugged. 'I know you're busy and, well, I suppose I didn't want to admit it to myself. I've had a good run at things really.'

'There are things we can do,' Cathy said. 'Please take your time.' She drew the curtain around the woman, having indicated that she should get dressed once more. She washed her hands absent-mindedly, dropping the paper towel in the pedal bin by the sink. The lid fell with a clang. From her desk now, she continued to speak. 'Can I ask how long it's been there – the lump?'

She heard the old woman sigh from behind the curtain as she paused getting dressed. 'Too long to remember. Months, maybe. I know I'm the very worst kind of patient. I should know better.'

'You used to be a nurse, you said?' Cathy asked as she typed in the lady's notes. *'Left lateral upper quadrant breast lump. Hard, craggy, irregular. 4cm approx. Skin dimpling, Erythema. No nipple discharge. Unilateral lymphadenopathy. URGENT BREAST CLINIC REFERRAL.'*

'Oh, many moons ago,' the woman said, now coming around the curtain. Mrs Scott slowly fussed with the curtain, setting it against the wall and then turned, and moving back to the bed, tore off the sheet of thin paper that had covered it, and drew another from the roll at the end of the bed.

'Oh, please, don't bother,' Cathy said, but it was clear that the woman wanted to.

She then settled herself in the chair beside the doctor's desk, fiddling with the handle of her handbag. 'Make the worst patients, so they say,' the old lady repeated.

Cathy nodded but didn't smile. 'I'll refer you up to the breast clinic as a matter of urgency. You'll be seen in the next day or so I expect. They'll do scans and see what's what. I assume you agree to that, so we can judge what we're dealing with?'

The woman raised her hands in acceptance. 'If you say so. I won't have treatment though. I've decided.'

'Let's see what they say first,' she said. 'Then we can talk about the pros and cons of treatments and all of the options. Many people initially feel the way you do but you'd be surprised how much things have changed over the years. The treatments now ...'

The woman nodded but Cathy felt that her words were falling on deaf ears.

'You came in last week and tried to see me on Friday,' she said, looking up having finished typing. 'Was it about this? I feel dreadful if you'd wanted to be seen but were too uncomfortable to say why. I'd have made the time to see you, or one of the other doctors ...'

But the old woman was shaking her head and smiling. 'No, I needed to see you. And in truth, the lump was just an excuse, I'd have left it longer really,' she said.

Cathy raised her eyebrows.

'No, my real reason for coming in today was to talk to you about a little issue at the charity shop.'

Cathy, now quite incredulous, smiled, and the elderly woman, with a twinkle in her eye, smiled back through her white halo of fringe.

## 3

'Well darling, what do you think? We'd go as a threesome obviously. I know you hate walking into things on your own. After a few drinks, it'd be fine though.'

Cathy had arrived home an hour later than she should have. She moved the mobile phone to her other ear as she opened the fridge door. Milk, eggs, margarine, and a rather out-of-date-smelling block of cheese. There was always omelette but perhaps she'd just have cereal and save herself the hassle. Her kitchen was rarely utilised. She could barely remember when she last had anything in the oven other than frozen pizza. It was the result of living alone for too long, she mused. Her last boyfriend had gone not long after her initial diagnosis of bipolar, unable to take any more of the rows and mood swings. She couldn't blame him. Since he'd gone, she had found, if not comfort in being alone, then acceptance of it. Now her social calendar only had in it meetings with insistent and stubborn friends who refused to be blocked-out. Suzalinna, her closest, and the only one who dared had been harping on about her getting back on the dating scene again, but Cathy felt that this was so far removed from where she was emotionally, it was almost laughable.

'Well?'

Cathy groaned. 'Oh, God, but why do we have to do it at all?' she asked. 'You know I hate these bloody things, Suz. Can't we just be happy to have kept in touch with the important friends from our year, in other words, each other, and go out for a meal ourselves without all the rest of them? Medic reunions are a well-known pain in the backside. Everyone will get pissed and talk about themselves and how many lives they've managed to save since we last saw one another. Then, there'll be the nerds who never intended on doing the degree to see patients. They'll huddle together and bore everyone with their vital research projects. Honestly, it'll be torture.'

Cathy heard her friend snort. 'You're awful,' Suzalinna said. 'Why not come? It's always funny to see what everyone's been up to. Last time they organised a reunion, it was only five years after qualifying, and we were all still boasting about our bloody exam results. It'll be different this time. People have moved past that. I want to see what everyone's ended up doing. Don't you want to know where they all are? Remember Orange Clarissa?'

'Oh yes. I wonder if she's found a better match for her skin tone yet. Well, she's one I'll be avoiding. Odds on, she'll be a consultant by now, but only having slept her way to the top.'

'There you go, see? I knew you were interested. There were other nice people in our year if you care to remember, or has it been such a bad day at the office that you can only recall your medical school days through blood-tinted spectacles?'

It was Cathy's turn to snort. 'You know my spectacles are more likely to be snot-tinted. I'm not elbow-deep in gore like you and your A and E buddies.'

Suzalinna laughed, but she wasn't letting it drop. 'It's not even as if we'd need to travel far,' she continued. 'It's at The

Georges just outside town. Everyone else moved away. Only you, me and a handful of others stayed put. The least you could do is come and talk to poor, old Saj. You know he hates these big, social gatherings. The two of you can support one another while I find out all the gossip. Oh, please darling. Do it for me. I'm booking our tickets now.'

Cathy, knowing full-well that she was being bulldozed, made a few more reluctant noises. Suzalinna was used to getting her way. It had always been so. Now, as a well-respected, but unquestionably arrogant A and E consultant, it had only escalated.

In many ways, Cathy found herself envying her friend's situation. Suzalinna and her husband, a pathology consultant, were undoubtedly a perfect match. They had supported Cathy through the last turbulent year. It was Suzalinna who had taken her for an initial appointment to see a psychiatrist. Cathy's practice partners had become increasingly concerned about her behaviour at work; her irritability and her rash judgements in dealing with people. There had been complaints about her language and then she had been caught self-medicating. That was the last straw.

But it was all in the past now. Since then, she had been established on an antipsychotic regime which, after the first few months of teething troubles, was helping a good deal. Her life, the psychiatrist said, was going to be very different post-diagnosis. It would have to be. Suzalinna and Saj had encouraged her to find a routine. She had been advised to avoid excitement but even this, along with the medication, might not stave off future relapses. Cathy knew that herself. She also knew how fortunate she was to be able to practise medicine at all now, albeit under the watchful eye of her senior practice partner James, and occupational health.

Cathy sighed. 'I'm too tired,' and she must have sounded it. In the end, it was agreed that she would sleep on it. Promising to talk again soon, Cathy hung up. That was the issue really if she was honest. Everyone else at the reunion would be boasting about their great careers, but the illness had curtailed hers. She was no longer allowed to train registrars. The stress was going to be too much. Her supervisor, who now met with her at three-monthly intervals, had recommended that she consider dropping a session. So far, Cathy had ignored the suggestion. Sometimes she felt trapped by the disease. Part of her yearned for the old, manic days, the thrill of the euphoria. Since starting the medication, this had been blunted considerably. A bit of excitement was what she craved. Perhaps Suzalinna was right, after all. She looked around her empty kitchen. The slog of the daily grind was enough to depress anyone. Impulsively, she snatched up her mobile.

'Go on then. Get me a ticket too.'

~

'I HAD an interesting one the other day, James,' Cathy said at coffee time the following day.

Dr Longmuir, Cathy's practice partner, now edging reluctantly closer to retirement, glanced sideways.

'Well?' he said, settling himself on one of the low, cushioned chairs along the edge of the upstairs room. In front of him, was a large pile of prescriptions waiting to be signed. Michelle had brought them up having printed them out at the front reception desk that morning, hoping that the GPs might get the opportunity to attend to them during their break. James moved the pink papers to the side and placed his mug of coffee on the table. 'Where's Linda anyway?' he asked. 'Shouldn't she be finished by now? I checked before coming up and there weren't any calls.'

'I popped my head in. She's catching up on lab results. Said she was bogged down,' Cathy said.

It had been a difficult few months for the practice, following the death of another doctor. It had been at the hands of one of their trusted team too and only because of Cathy's quick wit that the perpetrator was outed. It had been dreadful. Upsetting for everyone concerned and hard to steady the ship afterwards. The practice was unquestionably short on staff now. Linda, although less experienced and having returned only relatively recently to work following the birth of her second child, had stepped up to the mark. This had surprised both James and Cathy, as they had dismissed the girl as being somewhat of a dreamer and lacking in self-confidence, something that often seemed to lead to miscommunication with her patients. Cathy had struggled to warm to the younger GP but since the recent upheaval, they had become better acquainted. It was as well Linda had stuck around and accepted their offer of a salaried post. It meant that James and Cathy could relax for now.

'Anyway,' Cathy said, now coming across the room with her tea, and sitting opposite. She reached for the pile of prescriptions and patted her trousers. James shook his head and handed her his pen. Like most doctors who were required to sign a mountain of letters and prescriptions, Cathy had developed an initial, and a scrawl. She glanced up and smiled at her partner who watched on.

'Are you reading them?' he asked, and she laughed, then studying each paper, in turn, more carefully.

'Yes,' she said. 'Unusual one the other morning. Breast cancer. Very late presentation though,' she said. 'Quite sad really. Old lady. She's not been into me before. Not keen on treatment. Agreed to go to the breast clinic but that was it. Said she won't have surgery or chemo if they offer.'

'What was her name?' Dr Longmuir asked.

'Elizabeth Scott. Very much a do-gooder. Wanted me to help with some fundraising for the charity shop in the town. Very active still and all-there,' Cathy said, tapping her temple. 'It's funny, she wasn't as worried about the cancer as she was about drumming up donations. Strange though, I felt she was sizing me up, in a way. Testing me, almost to see if I'd do. I can't really explain it.'

'Scott,' James considered. 'Oh, yes, I do know who you mean. Betty Scott, of course. Used to be the matron up at Fernibanks.'

'Fernibanks? You mean the old psychiatric hospital?'

'Yes. And I thought she was long gone.' He chuckled. 'Must have been a tough job keeping a lid on some of them up at Fernibanks. She'll have been a tartar in her day no doubt.'

Cathy smiled and continued to scrawl her name but her hand grew tired and she paused to sip her tea. 'Are you going to help?' she asked, indicating the still-high pile of prescriptions.

'You've got my pen!' James remonstrated. 'So, what was the verdict then anyway?' he asked.

'What, the breast cancer? She had a backache. Maybe bony mets? It'll be past curative, I'd say.'

'No, about the fundraising. Are you going to go and do your bit for the community and help the nice charity shop ladies? Surely you've nothing better to do?'

Cathy snorted and threw the pen back at her partner. 'Your turn,' she said. 'As it happens, after negotiating Christmas with my parents, I've got a fifteen-year medical school reunion coming up in the new year. Goodness knows I'm a bit out of practice at this socialising nonsense though. I still need to get something to wear. Did you ever bother with the things? There's always one person in the year who takes it upon themselves to organise. I can't say I'm that keen.'

James nodded. 'Oh yes. The good old medic reunion. Fifteen years, eh? Oh, to be young again. I've kept up with a few. An old psychiatry pal, a surgeon who I used to golf with many years ago before wives and children took over. If our group have another one, it'll be less to see how classmates are, as much as to see who's still alive!'

Cathy smiled.

'It wouldn't do you any harm going to it though,' James continued. 'Get out and about a bit again, Cathy. It's been a rough year for you, I know, but time to start living again. Perhaps though, the charity shop's not such a great place to start. When I think about it, these places can be a hotbed for gossip. Middle-aged women who start work filled with altruism, and end up quite the opposite. Back-stabbing and poison. No, give that a miss. That's my advice.'

## 4

The bin bags were piled high that morning, as often they were on a Monday. Holly, slight of ankle and not uneasy on the eye, side-stepped two of them. But scooping up another bag in quite an unexpectedly wilful manner, she shouldered her way in, passing the darkened mannequins, their torsos wreathed in ill-chosen mismatches. She grimaced at her co-worker Carol, who scurried back to retrieve the rest.

Having deposited the bags in the back room, Carol returned to the front desk and sighed dramatically. 'Monday morning blues. I've been thinking all weekend about the fundraising ideas and I'm still no further forward. I wonder if anyone else has had any luck coming up with anything.'

Holly nodded but didn't answer.

'Betty's late in today,' Carol said, studying the diary. 'Doctor's appointment, I think. I hope nothing serious.'

Holly raised her eyebrows, and walked through to the back, removing her denim jacket and replacing it with one of the shop's navy tabards.

'We'll need to get on with the decorations today. That can be your job.' Carol followed her through.

Holly began to unpack one of the bags.

'Neil and Alex should be in soon,' Carol went on. 'It's a full-house once Betty comes back. As we're all in, I was going to pin people down about the Christmas meal. Have you thought about it yet?'

Holly momentarily looked skyward. 'I have,' she said. Her voice was surprisingly low and melodic. 'I think I said already that it was going to be tricky.'

'I know but it's not as if it's an evening. Just low-key. I checked the menu and it's only four pounds a starter. It'll be nice. A Christmas treat.'

Holly shook her head and continued to sort. She lifted a grey jumper from a heap of clothes on the floor and began to hang it up.

'Bobbling on it,' Carol said absentmindedly and darting forward, pointed to the chest of the garment and an infinitesimally uneven pile on the fabric.

Holly held it up, and smiled at an unvoiced joke, before tossing the offending article into the bag for recycling.

'Not the rag bag. The shop at Forkieth will take it. Anything substandard but reasonable goes to them. Put it in the green bag.'

Holly ignored her demands and continued to pick through the clothes. A tap at the front door signalled the arrival of another volunteer. Thankfully, Carol disappeared.

Holly had been working in the shop for six months now, having arrived in Glainkirk with little idea of what she was doing there. After the death of her father, and something of a breakdown in communication at home, she had settled herself in rented accommodation, at least for the short term. Families were complicated, and none more so than her own. It would be her first Christmas alone. Her mother had been texting her these past few days, begging her to return, even just for the day itself. Holly sighed. No, none of it was straightforward. But she was forced to put her melancholy thoughts aside as Tricia, a fellow volunteer, joined her. The two women sorted clothes in silence. Through the shop, Holly could hear Carol talking to a couple of early customers. The other volunteers appeared throughout the morning. Each popping their head around the door to say hello. The day began to creak into action.

At ten, Carol called for Neil to put the kettle on, and fluttering through, she lined up the mugs, all chipped donations now allotted to each of them.

The shop was quiet, as often it was following the morning surge. The co-workers gathered as usual and collected their steaming mugs. Carol took Betty her tea and a biscuit from the tin. The old woman had returned from her doctor's appointment not long before and had been stirring up trouble already. She had poked her head around the door and scolded Tricia for hanging two dresses the wrong way. 'Goodness Tricia. How long is it that you've been working here and you still can't get it right?' she had sneered, rolling her eyes. Tricia had blushed an ugly shade of crimson and hastily exited the room. Holly had heard her complaining to Carol about how unfair it all was, and really, she didn't need to continue working there when it was only voluntarily. Why should she, she whined, when she knew she'd have to put up with bullying daily? By coffee time though, things had settled and the workers pacified. Betty wouldn't join them for a break, which was just as well. She never did. Instead, she stayed ever-vigilant by the till. It was pointless really, but none of them argued.

The rest of them congregated now in the kitchen, leaning against the worktops. Holly found herself beside Neil, cramped up against the boxes of electrical goods that almost certainly wouldn't sell. Tricia was hovering by the door with Alex. Neil had been messing about with the tabletop that they rested against, and Holly felt it shift and wobble. He kept saying that he was going to bring his tools again in and fix it, but Holly doubted he ever would. She stepped forward and away from the swaying counter, distrusting it as much as the man beside her.

'Anything planned for Christmas?' he asked her.

It was just over two weeks until Christmas Day itself. Holly glanced around the kitchen. It was full to bursting with lovingly donated scraps of tinsel and outgrown elf costumes that no one would buy. That morning, after seeing too many bags of clothes, she had finally bowed to Carol's suggestion and had begun sorting baubles into sandwich-bags according to their colour. It was an utterly meaningless job, but oddly satisfying.

Holly took a sip of her tea. 'Usual,' she answered. 'What about you, Neil?'

'Family,' he said with equal nonchalance. 'It's not how it once was when they were small. Back when I had the shop on Broad Street, you know where I mean?'

Holly didn't know, but she nodded anyway.

The old man shifted and then propped himself back in position. The table juddered.

'Broad Street,' he said, shaking his head, clearly appreciating the memory of his heyday. His hair fell in grey, staccato barbs. He had allowed it to grow too long and beneath the haphazard fringe, his blue eyes flashed with pleasure. 'Some price it was for rent back then, but it was quite a place we had.' Neil looked at Holly now. 'Thirty-foot shed out the back,' he said. 'Thirty-by-twenty. Two of them, and the shop on two floors. Unbelievable really. You'd never find a place like that now. Nothing affordable anyway.'

Holly made an appropriate noise and continued to sip her tea, watching the man's face brighten in recollection.

'Reminds me of a dreadful thing, one Christmas though. The kids were only small back then. You'd be too young to remember,' he said. He looked instead at Tricia in the doorway. 'You remember that far back, Tricia? That trouble up at the loonies? All over the papers, it was and talk of the town for months on end.'

Tricia made an undecided attempt. 'Not sure if,' she began, 'was that when ...?'

Carol had since pushed her way into the small kitchen and stood cradling her mug.

'Betty's fine. She's had a custard cream,' she whispered. 'Worrying about her cat again.'

No one answered.

Neil smoothed the wooden top to the work-surface with his hand. Glancing across, Holly saw that his fingernails were slightly curved over the edge and unusually shiny.

'Long time ago,' he said. 'Terrible business it was too. Never heard of a violent death like it before, or since, thank God.'

Holly looked up. 'What happened?'

'Would've been near enough twenty years ago. No, hangabout, maybe not even as long as that, now I think about it,' he continued, drawing it out like the player he was. He paused, but this time Holly wasn't going to bite.

'Went in early that morning,' he finally said. 'Snow was like it always seemed to be back then in December. Winters were different. Harsh compared to now.'

There was a murmur of agreement from the older members of the crowd.

Neil shook his head. 'Can't believe none of you remember it,' he went on gleefully. 'Back then, I'd only had the shop a few years. I was new to the business see, and still learning the ropes? Six o'clock, I had gone in, Monday morning. Still dark and bloody freezing. Anyway,' he said, displaying his yellow tombstones. 'I had an odd feeling that morning as I went in. Closest I can describe it was like a chill going down my spine. I know you'll think it was just like I said; because it was so damn cold, but I tell you now, I had a feeling that there was something amiss.'

Holly glanced at the others, but none of them seemed in a position to argue.

'So, I go to open up as usual. I must have been one of the first folk out and about that morning. First to see it anyway. But goodness knows why no one saw or heard it before. A haze of smoke in the trees over the ledge of the hill. You know where the old loonie place is? Derelict now, half of it, but back then it was a grand, old place. Too big though. They had far too many odd buildings here and there. Must have cost a fortune to heat. Anyway, you know how it is? It's high enough up, but then the buildings dip behind a hollow, and then there are the trees too.'

Holly watched as Carol nodded impatiently. 'We know what you're talking about Neil. I wish you'd finish your story.'

Neil tutted. 'I suppose you *would* say that, after all,' he said. 'Anyway, I gave up on the shop, realising that something was wrong. I locked it up again, as I recall, and made my way up the hill through the drifting snow to take a look. Wish I hadn't if truth be told. What a mess! Only the one part, but dreadful. Totally burnt out and blackened, and the smoke rising. God knows how it didn't spread or catch onto another part, but there was only the one small building affected. There were inpatients, you see? Nurses and doctors stayed on-site too. No idea how no one alerted the fire brigade sooner, but I suppose it was one of the outer buildings, see? It was the one used for giving the folk electric shocks, so they say. Far away from the rest, so they never heard their screams.'

Carol shook her head. 'Don't be so sensational, Neil.'

'Was anyone injured?' Holly asked, her heart beating very fast.

Neil puffed himself up. 'One,' he said.

They all waited, and Holly wondered if she was the only one holding her breath.

'A man. Dead. Turned out he was one of the doctors. A psychiatrist. I forget his name. Not much missed by all accounts. All over the news, it was. Big inquiry too, but they never found out what happened that night, or why he was up there in the electric shock room. There was talk that he had been carrying on with one of the student nurses, but nothing came of that. Had a nasty reputation. Charred to a cinder, his body, and crushed under all the rubble. Dreadful mess it was, and stank for days after. The whole town was heavy with it.'

'So, you got the police?' Holly asked.

Neil grinned. 'I hurtled down that hill like nobody's business. Must've caught myself on some of the timber first though, and burnt my hand dreadful. Months afterwards I was still in pain with it and had to go and see that quack we had at the time, Doctor Fairweather. Think he was struck off,' he said, lifting the sleeve to his shirt and displaying a faded patch of skin. 'We had no phone back then and I had to jog down the high street to the police station. Rapped my knuckles raw hammering on their door until I got them up and out. Then they came, following me back up the road, and I showed them.' He broke off at this point and added to the act by mopping his brow with a folded handkerchief that he produced from his trouser-pocket.

They all waited, their tea growing cold, and the biscuits; long-forgotten.

'Things were different back then. No fingerprints, no video footage, or CCTV nonsense. Given up as a tragic accident it was. Dreadful thing really. Things changed up at that place after. I think they shut much of it and it became half-derelict.'

'So, they never found out why he was up there – the psychiatrist, I mean?' asked Holly. 'You said he'd been carrying on with one of the nurses? Do you mean an affair or something? Wouldn't she have been the first person to ask? Presumably, if there had been a liaison that night, she might have seen something?'

Neil laughed. 'Like I said, I don't know the ins and outs. They interviewed all sorts of folk. Don't suppose the doctor should have been up there at all, and maybe it was hushed up. You know how these medics like to close ranks?' Neil leaned back in satisfaction. 'So, what do you think of that?' he asked.

'It doesn't make any sense at all to me.' Holly said. Her hands had gone quite cold despite the lukewarm mug that she still clutched.

Neil seemed indifferent. 'Told you it was a good story,' he said.

The time for discussion had passed though, and the other volunteers were beginning to move away. Carol had already collected Tricia's half-drunk mug of tea and was placing it by the sink.

'You said there were other people actually on-site that night,' Holly persisted, refusing to move and forcing Carol to sidle past her.

'What, the patients?' Neil asked, picking up a string of tangled Christmas lights.

'Yes. But the other doctors and nurses. They could hardly leave a building burning all night and not call for help.'

'I told you. He'd been up to some mischief probably and they didn't want to get involved. Hushed up, you see? Probably a bad egg and deserved what he got.'

Holly left him to it. For the rest of that morning, she felt sick, and for once it wasn't because of the putrid bags of donations handed in.

5
———

Cathy prepared herself for a difficult discussion. She had read the letter from the specialist and had anticipated her patient's return this week. Elizabeth Scott walked along the corridor towards her. Cathy stood by the door, trying to judge the woman's mood. It was impossible to tell. The elderly lady busied herself, her steps small but animated if a little unsteady. She looked up at Cathy as she neared but didn't smile.

'Please take a seat.'

Elizabeth Scott sat down opposite and removed her woollen gloves, placing them tidily on top of her handbag.

'Quite some chill outside just now,' Cathy said, feeling it a safe opening gambit. 'I've been watching out my window and hoping no one falls on the ice rink.'

'That's your responsibility, you know?' the old woman said severely, and Cathy turned in surprise.

'You'll be sued if you don't put something down. Salt,' Mrs Scott said, shaking her head and tutting. 'And while we're on the subject, that receptionist. I don't know if you realise, but in the ten minutes I sat in your waiting room, she's been wasting your phone bill, gossiping. Half the room must have heard her giggling away. Highly unprofessional.'

James's words came back to her and at that moment, Cathy thought that her practice partner was probably quite right when he suggested that the old woman had been a tartar in her day.

'Anyway,' Cathy said, 'the hospital's been in touch, of course. But tell me how you got on.'

The woman shrugged. 'I knew it was bad. They poked and prodded a good deal as expected. I drew the line at them sticking a needle in me.'

Cathy smiled. 'Yes, the letter said. The fine needle aspiration would have helped to find out the tissue type and plan any treatment.'

The old woman was shaking her head. 'I told you before, and I told them too. I'm not interested.'

Cathy began to speak, but the elderly woman raised a hand. 'Please, let's not fall out, Dr Moreland. I like you far too much for that, and if, as you say, I'm short on time, I'd rather spend it in a useful manner.'

'What can I do? I'd like to support you the best I can.'

The old woman shifted in her seat, crossing her legs behind her and leaning forward. 'Well, if you'd like to adopt my cat?' she started, and then laughed down at her clasped hands. 'No, I'll not ask that of you. My neighbour. No doubt she will step in when the time comes. No, I'm trying to organise things, you see? Before it's too late. Things must be in order. The truth is, I'm very worried. Not about this,' she said fluttering a hand across her chest. 'But something's been on my mind a good deal. I've not known quite what to do about it for some time now, but all of this nonsense has forced my hand. I've no one of any use, you see, to go to about it? That's why I thought of you …'

Cathy withdrew her hands from the computer keyboard and gave the woman her full attention. 'What's concerning you?'

'You'll think I'm mad saying this, but I've been afraid.' The elderly eyes flickered, and Mrs Scott looked to the ceiling for a moment. 'I was happy to keep a check on it myself. I have been doing so, but I know that I may not be around for very long. It rather changes things, do you see?'

Cathy did not see, but now acutely interested, she leaned in.

'You cleared up that little mess over the other doctor's death, I hear?' the old woman continued. 'That's really why I chose you in the first place. Of course, I'm sure you're an excellent doctor also.' Her smile faded and she sighed.

Cathy waited.

'I don't want to be melodramatic, really I don't, but there's something in Glainkirk. It's not quite right.' She shook her head, perhaps trying to reframe her thoughts. 'Something disturbing,' she continued, more forcefully, 'if not, dangerous. I hope you don't think I'm some batty, old woman saying this. I think if you came into the charity shop, you might well see what I mean. I'm afraid, Doctor. Terribly afraid.'

## 6

Holly knew that her habit of being boastful and supercilious was the cause of all her trouble. From her earliest years, she had tried to impress. As she sat in her rented flat alone now, sipping her vodka, she cast her mind back. None had travelled as far as her or had as many wealthy relations. In her final year of primary school, she had announced to anyone who would listen that she was adopted and that her real parents were lesser-known members of the Indian aristocracy. All very hush-hush. Her father, who had fallen out with the rest of the family, had wanted her to be raised in a westernised society and had reluctantly sent her abroad. Being of a darker complexion than her very-Scottish mother, some of them had believed her. Holly smiled in recollection. Quite inventive given her age. She swilled the clear liquid around the glass and took another mouthful, grimacing as it tracked her oesophagus.

Secondary school had been different, of course. It became clear very quickly, that to survive in a rougher academy, she was far better to blend in and keep quiet. The exaggerations abruptly stopped then.

School was a bit of a disappointment on the whole and her home life wasn't much better. Very loving, without a doubt, but wrong in some way. Her parents were on the older side of average. Both had been incredibly proud of her natural intellect, which far exceeded that of anyone else in the family. Despite knowing it was unkind, she repeatedly found herself mocking her mother's gullible and gentle nature. The more entertainment she gained from this, the more self-disgust she suffered. It was like a vicious circle really.

In her school work, she found some solace. For her, to achieve top grades was undeniably easy. A cursory glance over her term's work was all it took. Teachers praised her understanding of the subjects; they told her parents that they saw great things in the future for her. But repeatedly, it was observed that she was aloof and a little snooty.

It was probably due to this generalisation, that she agreed to go out for an evening of underage drinking in the first place. Of course, no one had openly said that alcohol would be involved. The group simply arranged to meet at the swings after seven-thirty. Everyone knew though, that a couple of the kids' parents would turn a blind eye if a bottle of wine or a couple of cans of cider went astray. Holly arrived early with a rucksack full of booty. That evening would be when it would all change for her. Her reputation would be reformed and her character completely renewed. No more 'aloof' or 'snooty.' She would emerge from the park, like a butterfly from its chrysalis.

There was a tough girl called Lorraine who sat next to Holly in Biology class. Holly had passed her the answers in the last exam, partly because she was slightly afraid of her, but also because she had overheard the teachers whispering that Lorraine would be kicked out if she failed another. They had been at the park for over an hour. Lorraine was showing off a bit to the crowd, crushing beer cans with her fist and making smart remarks if anyone walked past. Up until then, all was going to plan. Holly had chatted quietly to the others and when the urge came to laugh at the incorrect things they said, she bit her tongue and smiled.

'Who's the biggest teacher's pet in the year?' Lorraine suddenly called out after taking a swig of her beer. Holly took no notice and continued talking to the girl beside her. Lorraine repeated the question, but louder and then came over to where she sat on one of the swings. She stood directly in front of her. 'Say it, Holly,' Lorraine insisted. 'Go on. Say: "I'm the biggest teacher's pet." Do it, stand up and tell them all.' By this time, the rest of the group had fallen silent. Holly said nothing. But when Lorraine leaned forward and touched her shoulder, she couldn't help herself. She leapt up from the swing and seized by ferocious anger that even she hadn't known existed, she punched the other girl hard in the stomach. Lorraine sank to her knees, winded and tearful. Holly had never punched anyone before and the shock of doing so was quite thrilling.

She took a long draught of her vodka now, as she reflected on the injustice of it all. The others might have respected her for standing up to the bully. Instead, they set on her, the whole lot of them. She scratched and spat at them, but didn't stand a chance. Holly closed her eyes as the memories swam. She felt quite nauseous. What they did to her was more humiliating than painful, but when she crept back home and showered, she was unable to disguise the rainbow of bruises from her mother. 'Fell off the swings,' she lied and retreated to bed.

The secret drinking began not long after the park incident. Holly knew that her parents were aware. Too compassionate, she mused. They'd put it down to a teenage phase, and did nothing to prevent her from continuing. Her grades slipped at school. Holly snorted now at the irony. If she had been renowned for her aloofness once, she grew even more so after that.

In the end, it was her chemistry teacher who had had a word. He asked her to stay back after class and shut the door. 'Too clever to throw it all away,' he had said with genuine feeling. 'Time to think about life after school.' One thing, in particular, had stuck in her mind. He had said that the people she knew now, weren't her 'tribe'. None of them was a bit like her. She would only find a genuine belonging if she dug deep and got away from the place. The only way was to get the exam results she deserved, and that meant effort.

In many ways, Holly thought that Mr Robinson had saved her that day. His words had been strangely accurate too. Odd how things turned out though, she considered, coming to the bottom of her glass. But there was no point overthinking. Perhaps a top-up was in order. It was early still, after all.

# 7

'Bloody heck, it's hot in here isn't it, ladies? You sure you still need the heater on?' Neil looked into the back room and grinned.

It was the week following New Year, and after a five-day break, they had all returned. Holly had despaired when she arrived. The wooden frame which housed all of the bags was near to full.

Neil continued past the doorway. 'Nice Christmas and Hogmanay?' he threw over his shoulder but didn't wait for an answer.

She turned to see Tricia scooping a belted pencil skirt from the mound of clothes on the floor. 'Oh pretty,' the other woman said, attempting to attach the garment to a hanger. It seemed that following an hour of blissful silence, now warmed up both physically and mentally, Tricia was ready to converse.

'So, you've not told me about your Christmas,' she said, still fiddling with the hanger and accidentally allowing the skirt to fall to the floor in a heap.

'Usual,' Holly said non-committally. 'Too much food and drink.'

In truth, the break had been dreadful, but Holly wasn't ready to reveal anything so personal to her co-workers. If they knew the extent of her loneliness, she felt sure that they would attempt to console her, if not engage her in their social activities, and Holly could imagine nothing worse.

Further comment was halted thankfully, due to a commotion in the front shop. Holly and Tricia looked at one another, hearing Carol's voice raised. Tricia crossed the small room and peered around the corner. Holly stayed where she was, listening.

'I'm not!' Carol was saying. 'I've explained, it makes more sense that way. Every time I make a suggestion ...'

Holly couldn't hear the reply, so she joined Tricia in the doorway and was just in time to see Betty leaning over the front desk and pointing. 'Don't use that tone with me,' she was saying. 'This nonsense over the till. When will you get it into your head? Sometimes I wonder if you're fit to be in charge. I see you bossing them around.' She fluttered a hand in the direction of the back room. Tricia shrank back.

'Are you actually afraid of her?' Holly asked.

The other woman laughed. 'Heavens no. I just don't like arguments, that's all.'

Holly leaned out again as Betty was jabbing a finger at Carol's tunic. It was odd to see the transformation. On the outside, Betty was just like any other old biddy; harmless and a bit unsteady on her feet. But looking at her now, she was quite something to behold. She'd seen Betty in action on a couple of occasions since she'd started work there. Usually, it was an argument over who should be operating the till, as it indeed seemed to be now. There seemed always a bubbling undercurrent and occasionally, the pressure became too great. Then, either Carol or Betty would blow.

This time, Betty did seem determined to stand her ground. Holly watched in wonder, comparing Betty to a creature from

Greek mythology she had read about years ago. The harpy was half woman, half bird of prey. A grasping monster. Holly smiled. The old woman's eyes, usually a haze of cataract had now altered and were piercing. Her fingers were splayed like talons, and her voice; hissing and spiteful.

'Not with me,' she was saying. 'I'm old, but I'm not stupid. None of you should forget it.'

Sadly, the stand-off was prevented from further escalation by Neil. Having failed to overhear the dispute, he cheerfully called through and looking at the clock, it seemed that it was indeed 'cuppy time'. But before Holly could step outside the room, he was in the doorway.

'Thought you'd like a look,' Neil said, barely able to contain his pleasure. 'Would've shown you earlier but it went out of my head.'

This, Holly felt sure was a lie. No doubt, he had been sitting on his little surprise, just waiting for the right moment.

He handed her a piece of newspaper. Its folds had been stressed by time, and the paper was so delicate and grainy as to twist and almost fracture with her touch. It had been cut with the precision of a surgeon. She held the translucent piece in her hand, knowing already what it was.

'What we were talking about the other day before Christmas,' he said in explanation, scuffing the side of his shoe, as was his habit.

'Right,' Holly said and looked down again. The paper was yellowed and the newsprint faded. The words were slightly offset in places, giving the article a drunken slant.

'DEATH AT FERNIBANKS HOSPITAL' the title read. Holly scanned the bare facts, knowing that his eyes were on her, and despising him for it.

'Thanks,' she said and handed it back as if it were the most tedious thing she had ever seen.

'Thought you'd like to see,' he said. 'I'll pass it around. Maybe show it to Carol.'

He moved back along the corridor to the kitchen. The kettle was vibrating on its stand. Holly glanced across at Tricia.

'Coming?' she asked, not caring a bit one way or another. Her hands were shaking and she hoped that Neil hadn't seen.

She was aware of Neil moving back through the corridor with a mug of tea for atrocious Betty, who still refused to be pried from her beloved till. Holly paused in the doorway and watched him, ingratiating and jovial even with the old woman. He handed Betty the mug, which she positioned at the side. Then, reaching into his pocket, he produced the scrap of newsprint. Holly wasn't sure what happened at that moment, perhaps he jogged her elbow and knocked it, but within seconds, Carol, who had obviously forgiven Betty, was swooping in and about, and hastily mopping up the spilt, hot liquid. Repeatedly, she checked that Betty hadn't burnt herself, and generally made a fuss.

Neil returned to Holly with an air of indifference.

'Looked like she'd seen a ghost,' he said. 'I thought she was having a stroke for a second.' Chuckling, he returned to the kitchen once more.

In truth, Holly had thought of little else since she had heard his story. Even though the period should have been festive, she had found her mind returning continually to the grisly tale. Over the past few days, she had begun to wonder if the whole thing had been a charade, a misconstrued, befuddled memory, twisted and embellished over time. She had chastised herself for being so gullible but now she had seen the evidence in newsprint, it must be so.

It was a relief when her four-hour shift ended that late-afternoon and she was freed from the confines of the back room. Following Carol's strict and pathetic protocol of signing-out in the spiral notebook kept behind the front desk, she found herself wandering without any real purpose. Neil's story was still very much on her mind as she walked.

The Glainkirk high street was pretty rundown by anyone's standards. It seemed to Holly that the charity shop was, in a way, the heart of the community. Here, locals gathered and conversed, if not in the shop itself, then outside by the postbox and bus stop.

Carol had told her that times had changed. Since Carol had started working in the shop (and that must have been more than ten or fifteen years ago), she said that the tide had turned. Whether it be due to necessity or fashion, people were now willing to pay for second-hand goods, as long as they were of reasonable quality. Carol also reliably informed her that they were one of the more affluent shops in the area. She believed it was because of the parking outside. In reality, it was a bus stop and not an actual parking space, but it did allow people to offload their bags before hoofing it back to the car and driving away. Sometimes, they seemed embarrassed to be caught in the act of depositing a bag, and at other times, they wanted heartfelt thanks for this act of generosity.

It had rained during the day and the pavements still shone. Before Holly had thought about what she was doing, she had walked the entire length of the high street and had turned inexplicably left rather than right. Given that she was in no hurry to return to her empty flat, she instead continued, walking slowly towards the railway line. She looked into the windows of the houses that she passed, seeing that the Christmas-tree lights that had shone garishly before, had all been packed away.

As she neared the bottom of the street, the houses petered out. Some of the residents seemed to have used the scrap of wasteland as a makeshift dump. An elongated mound of grass cuttings and leaves was heaped at the side. The railway line lay beyond. Some of the grasses, although dead or dying, remained high. The architecturally intricate umbellifers, now naked of their flowers, reached upwards to the sky, like despairing hands.

The afternoon was turning to evening far earlier than it should. A wind had picked up and brought with it a chill of fine mist. Head down, she marched onwards, a little unsure as to where this route might come out. She was almost turning back in the direction of the high street once again when the jangle of live rails began. Instead, she waited. The rails sang louder. The train swept into sight and the breeze lifted further, buffeting her backwards, making her lose balance slightly and step away. Once past, she followed the lights as it wound its path out of the town and towards the open fields, convoluting and writhing through farmland and countryside.

Holly shook her head. What was she doing here anyway? Shouldn't she be on that train, travelling north, back to her real home? She plunged her hands deep into her pockets and began to walk once more. The flats on either side were rundown and neglected. She came level with what must once have been a shop. The windows were now boarded, the mesh-wire rusted and graffitied. She looked up towards the end of the street. A sign was positioned at the corner and she could only just make out the words. Broad Street. Of course. She had inadvertently fallen upon the place where Neil had once had his old antique shop.

She found herself looking then upwards to the embankment that Neil had described. Above and to the right, lay the old psychiatric hospital. Impulsively, Holly changed course and plunged knee-deep into the damp grasses. The hill was steep, and at times, she had to lean forward and grab at the grass to gain better purchase. Finally, breathless and in awe, she stood and surveyed the carcass of the old building. The perimeter of the ruined hospital was now fenced, with signs displayed at regular intervals threatening potential intruders that the land was patrolled regularly, and trespassers would be prosecuted. The buildings themselves loomed dark and imposing.

She stood for some time considering the scene. The tragedy had clouded her thoughts ever since hearing of it. It had become an obsession with her. Even standing there, despite not knowing in which building it had occurred, she could sense the horror of that day. All those years ago. This was why she had come to Glainkirk. The charity shop, she had known was important, but it was in the crumbling wreckage of the old hospital, where her answers lay, long since buried with the charred embers of that terrible night.

# 8

Cathy pulled up the top of her dress for the umpteenth time as she stood at the top of the steps.

'Stop fidgeting. I'll keep a lookout in case you expose yourself in public if that's what's worrying you.'

She gave her friend a withering look, and the two women, accompanied by a very dapper-looking Saj, walked into the hotel.

She hadn't found a chance to speak to Suzalinna about her troubling consultation the previous week. In truth, Cathy had gone about her business, still stunned by what Mrs Scott had said, and perhaps a little disbelieving. At the time, she had tried to push for more information, but Elizabeth Scott would not disclose names or go into detail. She said that she needed to talk it through with the person concerned. They had had a fine time of things, she said, but now that she was dying, she said that she couldn't leave this world with the injustice of it still burdening her.

'You are my insurance policy. I have no intention of dying sooner than I have to, but I'm no fool, and I realise I've only got months rather than years. I feel happier knowing that I've at least spoken to someone. It's the charity shop, you see? That's where the worry lies. I'm old. Perhaps I've been too weak. I've allowed it to go on for far too long. If you'd just take a look, I'm sure you'd understand.'

Cathy didn't know what to say. Before leaving, Mrs Scott had asked once more if she would at least agree to the fundraising. There was a new year's tombola and they were looking for donations. If a highly respected member of the community came and drew the winning tickets it would undoubtedly be an advantage. She must have seemed hesitant because when she looked up, the old lady's expression was anguished and her eyes watery.

'I don't think you quite understand,' she had said in a choked whisper.

Cathy raised her eyebrows.

'I'm not one for melodrama, believe me, but I was a nurse. Please, Doctor. Please believe me when I say that I remember things even now. Oh Lord, if you knew! But I can't talk like this. I told myself I'd give them their chance to do the right thing. If they won't, if they refuse,' Mrs Scott said, her voice dropping, 'I must ask, I must beg, that you'll help. I might not have it in me.'

Cathy could make little of this, but before Betty left, the old woman had composed herself once more.

'Thank you for your understanding,' she smiled weakly. 'It would put my mind at rest, far more than I can tell you if you'd come. Don't let it trouble you for now though. I need to approach the interested party first, and then I'll talk again.'

But Cathy had worried, as anyone in her position might. She had worried about what Betty Scott had said. The whole consultation had been very unsettling. What on earth had she meant by 'disturbing and dangerous?' Cathy's brow furrowed in recollection.

∽

'Smile,' Suzalinna said, cutting into her thoughts. 'I promise it won't be that bad.'

They had taken a taxi to the place. The Georges was a little out of town. Perhaps three miles or so; a country retreat that had once probably belonged to some Lord or other, but had more than likely cost too much to maintain as a family home. The drive, lit on either side at regular intervals by lanterns, swept up to the building, which itself was accented, by orange up-lighters.

As they handed in their jackets, Cathy decided that she must put her concerns over the old lady's story to the back of her mind for that night at least. She had already spotted several groups of well-heeled people. Most of the women wore dresses either decorated by sequins or velvet. Everyone seemed to be clutching a glass of champagne and talking excitedly.

'Oh shit!' she hissed, suddenly recognising a face. 'Look who's over there.'

Suzalinna laughed. 'Not changed much, has she? Come on, we'd better go and say hello until someone more interesting arrives.'

In the end, the evening wasn't so bad. They had been seated at a table with five other medics, several of whom Cathy couldn't remember, probably because they had only joined the class in their third year when all of the students were beginning to do work placements. To the left of Cathy though, was a girl she had known, called Sally. It turned out that she had moved down to London and was now a respiratory consultant in a large teaching hospital.

'Funny, looking around at all of us now we're grown up,' the woman said to Cathy.

'I know,' Cathy said. 'I feel like a fraud still. Imposter syndrome.'

Sally laughed. 'I get that all the time. Half of my foundation year twos know more than me because they're swatting up for college exams.'

'Are you married now then?' Cathy asked. 'Weren't you dating someone all through Uni? I forget his name. Wasn't it Alexander, or am I thinking of someone else?'

The woman laughed. 'I can't believe you remember. Yes, but we split up. He wasn't keen on London when we moved down together, and his work was taking him in a different direction. I think he quit the police in the end,' she said. 'No idea what happened to him. I am married now though. Two kids. Twins. Bloody nightmare, but London's very different. It's not unusual to get in nannies. We've got a Romanian girl living with us. Chris works away a good deal. Pharmaceuticals. I know,' she laughed at Cathy's expression. 'He hates it, but the money's good. He's a medic too but went over to the dark side in an advisory role. What about you? Husband? Kids?'

At that point, the conversation was interrupted. A flashy-looking and distinctly orange woman came over from another table.

'Suzalinna! Cathy! All these years and look at you both. Still thick as thieves.'

'Hi Clarrisa,' Suzalinna said rather coldly. 'How's life then?'

'Fabulous darling,' Clarrisa said and laughed. Every inch of her seemed to glitter, it was like she'd sprayed herself in the stuff. 'How's A and E anyway?' she asked. 'I heard you were the first in the year to get a consultant post. Well done. I took longer. Got my membership to the college the second time though, which isn't bad. I think most give up after the fifth attempt at the surgical entrance exam. Everyone knows they have to make the surgery assessments more rigorous though, obviously.'

'Oh, so you went for surgery then, did you?' Cathy asked.

Clarrisa turned and swept her blonde mane of hair back

over her shoulder. 'Oh, surgery from the start darling. I was sure.'

'You were keen on gastro, I remember,' Cathy said.

An expression of annoyance flashed across Clarissa's heavily made-up face. 'Ancient history. Bloody medics,' she said shortly. 'Married a surgical professor in York. You were paddling about in GP-land though, I seem to remember. Nice. Not unexpected. Heard you'd not been so well though recently.' Before waiting for a response, she turned back to Suzalinna once more.

Cathy rolled her eyes at Sally. 'Nothing changes,' she mouthed, and her comrade laughed.

'What did she mean about you being unwell?' Sally whispered.

'Oh, I've no idea how she heard, but you know what gossip's like. Bipolar. I took some time out and I'm thankfully back at work again these last few months.'

The woman nodded. 'It's very real. Mental illness amongst doctors. I don't think we look after ourselves well enough. Back in our junior house-officer days, do you remember how harshly you'd be looked upon for taking a single day off sick? It was as if you were dumping on the rest of the team.'

Cathy laughed. 'Not just that, but the ward rounds.' Cathy looked skywards. 'Oh, the pressure of having everything in perfect order for the consultant.'

'My rounds aren't like that,' Sally reassured her.

'I'm glad to hear it, but it used to be par for the course to be ritually humiliated in front of a surgical consultant. Remember the guy who used to throw folders at us when we got the answers to his questions wrong?'

Sally laughed.

'Tough times. I'm sorry you've been unwell though,' she said. 'I remember during our psychiatry block, the lecturer saying that out of our year, at least two would end up being schizophrenic, many more: bipolar, and almost all of us would have undiagnosed personality disorders.'

Cathy smiled. 'I remember that too.'

She looked around the room, a sea of glowing faces. All brilliant, intelligent people, all making a difference to the world. All apparently living altruistic, fulfilled lives. Cathy wondered as she watched the others laughing around her, how many were, in reality, struggling to stay afloat. She thought again of her worrying patient. How many people were there out there? People, who superficially looked normal, but were in fact, concealing something? If Elizabeth Scott was to be believed, then someone in Glainkirk was pretending to be quite ordinary, but the old woman had perceived something unusual. Something warped and distorted. Cathy hoped with all her heart that she was wrong.

## 9

'When did you say it was again?' Holly asked, stalling for time.

Carol looked at her with obvious exasperation. 'The eighth. Wednesday. I've already checked prices and it's only four pounds for a starter and seven for a main. It's quite low-key.'

Holly looked around the kitchen. It was a chaos of boxes, stacked high on the shelves. A transparent, plastic container beside her held crockery, the old-fashioned kind. The edge of the plates was rimmed with chipped gold-paint. Finally, her eyes settled on Carol's mouth. Her lips had receded. All but disappeared with age, and her mouth was dry. The skin around it; puckered and wrinkled, sucking her teeth inwards. Perhaps she would eventually swallow herself.

'Carol,' she said definitely, trying to suppress a smile. 'I've not been here that long ...'

'Alex's coming.'

Holly sighed. 'Sure, put my name down,' she said, but both of them knew that she had no intention of going. 'I'll go home and check my diary.'

'It's this coming week,' Carol said desperately, 'I need a definite ...'

The back room was like a safe-haven in contrast to the torture of the kitchen interrogations. Carol had had a bee in her bonnet over the ridiculous meal for what seemed like weeks. It had been going on since well before Christmas. Even lumpy Tricia, who had agreed initially, said that it was going to be awkward. A little celebratory meal, Carol had repeated. Just a small thing. At first, Holly had thought she meant that the charity was paying, but when she began listing prices, and quoting options on the menu, her heart sank. Not that she would have gone anyway, even if it had been for free. After much toing and froing over dates (Betty was tied up with her church group on Thursdays, Tricia had her old folks' home and her befriending on Tuesdays or Saturdays, or something) the pre-Christmas assembly had been abandoned. Holly had celebrated hearing this, only to be disappointed by Carol's later announcement; that she planned to organise another event in the new year.

All in all, the morning hadn't gone as planned. She had hoped to leave the shop early and make a short trip to Forkieth to do some research. The draw of the library felt like an ache now. Despite turning her back on her studies, she still felt that in whatever town she ended up, it was here, surrounded by books, that she could feel at home.

Almost as soon as she had arrived at work however, she was disappointed. Signing in, she saw that both Neil and Alex were away, and Betty had scored a line through her name for that afternoon, with 'hospital appointment' scrawled in a tremulous, spidery hand. Another one? Perhaps something was wrong with the old woman after all. She had been watching Betty more recently, noting her wide gait and shrinking frame. Maybe her suspicions were correct. She had always been good at noticing details, she'd often been told that.

Carol had explained from the beginning that the shop needed at least three people to be there at all times, and she required plenty of notice if people couldn't come in. Holly did wonder for a second or two if she might force upon Carol the indignity of shutting up shop early. They were volunteers after all with no obligation to stay in the place if they didn't want. She could easily feign illness. She knew all of the symptoms to make it just a little too uncomfortable for Carol to ask any detailed questions. But Holly supposed that part of her, although keen to do her research, recognised that the implications might be enormous. Perhaps, in a way, she was fearful of finding the specifics about the psychiatric hospital horror too easily. She thought of the papers on her kitchen table. She had turned them over and over since her father's death. God knows how her family thought they could keep the truth from her. Just a first name. Elizabeth. Just a place. She'd never even been to Glainkirk before, not once. No one had mentioned the place in her whole life. Why there and who had it been? An inpatient? A nurse? The fire coinciding with the date seemed too much to ignore. Maybe that was why she didn't push to leave early that day. It was why she had come here, but she was afraid of what she might find.

As it turned out, her day was eventful anyway. Carol, having become incensed by multiple trips to the council dump with her own car, had apparently persuaded the charity bosses to agree to the hire of a private skip, hoping that they might clear some of the larger, more cumbersome items that simply wouldn't shift.

The skip-hire company had not confirmed a date or time for delivery, and to Carol's obvious dismay, they arrived unannounced and, on a morning, when she was short-staffed with only Betty and Holly, with her.

'We can't leave only two in the shop. It's against the rules,' Carol said to the driver, who stood by the front desk holding a paper for her to sign. 'I'll have to ...' She looked around wildly.

Betty was, as always, by the till. She smiled nastily, apparently enjoying the other woman's dilemma.

Carol's frantic gaze fell on Holly.

'Just show them where you want it. You're only going out for five minutes for God's sake, Carol.'

Carol looked torn for a second, but the driver, a burly Neanderthal, was picking up a loosely packed box of Christmas cards from the front desk, disturbing Carol's carefully crafted display. This seemed to settle it.

'I'll be quick,' Carol said, moving suddenly. She paused for a moment and clutched onto the desk.

Holly, despite her dislike for the woman, took a step forward, fearing that Carol might be about to faint. 'Sit down a second. Your blood pressure dropped,' she said.

'Just moved too quickly,' Carol said, her face insipid. 'It happens. Old age.'

Carol scuttled through the shop, and returning from the back with her winter coat, dived out, followed by the brute.

'Postural hypotension,' Holly muttered under her breath, but no one heard.

The shop fell silent. She and Betty looked at one another. They rarely conversed. Holly marvelled at Betty's continued obstinacy, coming in day-after-day, despite Carol's repeated attempts to overthrow her from her preferred position. They stood there for some time. Holly studied Betty's hunched shoulders, her face; crumpled and worn. She wondered what kind of life must have led to so many lines. What sights had those clouded eyes seen?

The old woman shrugged, as if in answer to her unvoiced question, accepting their lack of communication without the embarrassment of youth. Oddly, it didn't trouble Holly either. She felt as if she could stand wordlessly forever. Rarely did one get an opportunity to study someone with their full complicity.

The old woman blew a strand of hair that had rested on her forehead upwards, parting the corner of her creased mouth to do so. She cleared her throat; a reedy rasp of phlegm. Holly wondered if Betty was gravely unwell. She waited. Her mouth was dry. Instead of speaking, Betty produced from below the front desk, several plastic bags. Slowly and methodically, she laid them out on the desk, and taking the first, she began folding the cellophane over and over. She re-met Holly's gaze and a smile pricked her non-existent lips. Her hands, although feeble, moved with assurance. Holly watched, mesmerised. She wished she could reach out and touch, to feel the gnarled and twisted junctions of her wrists and fingers.

Holly wondered if Betty had known of the tragedy at the hospital before Neil had shown her the paper. She thought that she probably had. She wished she could ask. Instead, she stood watching. Perhaps the old woman thought she was shy, or mentally deranged. Maybe Holly was both of these things. She wanted the moment to never end.

'We need to talk. You know that, don't you?' Betty finally said. Her voice came like miasma through gravel. 'I know more than you think. You've come looking for answers, but you're playing a very dangerous game, young lady.'

Holly stood completely still. The thump of her heartbeat rang in her ears. Could it really be her? Betty was short for Elizabeth. Holly wasn't sure if she voiced the words or not.

The old woman blinked slowly.

But the spell was broken. Carol reentered the shop in a flurry of anxious energy.

Holly hated Carol more than ever that day.

## 10

'You're dripping,' Carol called after her. Holly turned to see a trail of brownish liquid exuding from the bag. She hurried through to the back, her stomach lurching.

It was the day following the staring match and Holly felt that she and Betty really must finally speak. She had come in determined to have it out with the old woman. But as yet, she hadn't appeared.

'Gloves for those, I think,' Carol called through. 'Might have been sitting in a puddle on the doorstep, and we only just bleached the floor last night. I'll have to do it again.'

It was gone half-past nine when Carol began to express her growing concerns over Betty, who had still to appear. If Holly was honest, she too had begun to worry, not that she would have said.

'It's so unlike her. You know how she is. Usually, so punctual, and she'd always ring to say if she was held up. I hope it wasn't bad news at the hospital the other day.'

Holly knew that if it did indeed turn out to be bad news, and she suspected it might, Carol would enjoy nothing more than to revel in Betty's misfortune.

'She's probably slept in, for once in her life. Have you phoned?'

Carol said that she had, twice.

'Well, go around if you're that worried. Neil's meant to be coming into work in an hour, isn't he? And Alex is here. Tricia and I will manage fine with the till if that's what's worrying you.'

'I don't like to just go to the house,' Carol said pathetically, wiping her perfectly clean hands on the front of her tabard.

Holly wondered if she was suggesting that either Tricia or she should go and check. But there was no way she was doing it.

In fact, Holly knew exactly where the old woman lived having followed her home a good number of times. She knew where most of her co-workers lived. It was a bit of a game she liked to play. It appealed to her sense of adventure, to shadow them without being seen. Betty had been her quarry on several occasions and only living five minutes away, it made for a quick and rewarding hunt.

'How was the bag anyway?' Carol asked a little later.

'The wet one?' Holly asked. 'I barely touched it. It was soaked through, so I just re-bagged the lot and threw it in the skip out the back. It couldn't even go in the rag bag. All filthy.'

∼

THOMAS WAS one of their regulars. A man in his late fifties, with a learning disability but plenty of chat. He came in frequently for 'a news' as he called it, and ended up hanging about the place causing trouble, more often than not. Even when he did leave the shop, he would stride up and down outside by the bus stop. Sometimes, he stopped passersby and accused them of being his uncle's brother, or his mother's dentist, or some such nonsense. Occasionally, if things were quiet in the shop, Holly would cast an eye outside to see if Thomas was preventing customers from entering.

On more than one occasion, Tricia or Carol had been forced to shoo him away, especially if he was in a particularly boisterous mood. Holly, against her better judgement, rather liked his resolve and ignorance of social etiquette. He had no self-awareness whatsoever and seemed impossible to demoralise.

His trips to the charity shop had become so frequent that it seemed that they were as much a part of his routine now, as any of the other social work-organised activities that filled his week. Several times, he had suggested that he also volunteer, but they all knew that that couldn't happen.

Usually, Thomas came into the shop around lunchtime, to avoid bumping into his arch-enemy Carbolic, another troubled gentleman who frequented the shop from time to time. Carbolic was, of course, not the man's real name. Although, it was what they all called him, and to his face too, not that he minded. Holly believed his name was Frank, but she couldn't be sure. She had once asked Carol why they called him this, and in telling her, Carol revealed something about herself that Holly had not known.

'I had dealings with him professionally years and years ago,' she had said, whilst folding a donated duvet cover. As she held it up, her arms outstretched, she almost completely disappeared behind the mauve and pale-green, flowered print.

For the first time, Holly considered a different Carol, a person who had once had a life.

'What did you do?' Holly asked.

'Oh, didn't I say? Social work.'

Holly was dumbfounded, and she tried to imagine Carol in this role, but couldn't.

'He was one of our trickier customers,' she went on, unaware of Holly's surprise. 'Although it wasn't my area of expertise, and I was only looking after him briefly as holiday cover. I never managed to help the man much. Such a shame. Full of anger. Sometimes, I thought he'd hit one of us when we went around. He's mellowed with age though,' she said almost sadly. 'Not half the man he once was.'

'What happened?' Holly asked, refolding a pillowcase for the third time.

'Well, even I don't know what made him the way he was, but he lived an almost feral life. You used to see him going up and down the street and avoid him. His house was down by the railway lines. It's boarded up now. Goodness knows how many years he lived in that place, hoarding rubbish. His family doctor went in to find him with no heating, no running water. Rats everywhere. You could hardly move for the mountains of litter he had kept. Bag upon bag of rotting food or junk, although of course, he didn't see it that way. He thought it was treasure.'

Holly must have looked enthralled because the other woman went on.

'That's when we went in, but as I say, I never managed to persuade him to allow us to clean it up. He stayed up at the old hospital for a while, I recall. A few years after I had left the job, he had another health scare, I think. Had to go into hospital again, and that's when social work saw their chance. The neighbours, you see? Rats everywhere.'

Holly nodded.

'So, they transferred him temporarily to The Court.' (By this she meant the sheltered housing complex down the road. It housed a good twenty or so residents with additional needs. Thomas was one of them also. Holly supposed it was how the two of them had met.) 'Said it was just to recuperate, I believe,' Carol continued, 'but he never had the option to return to his own home. It was harsh, I agree,' she said, clearly reading her thoughts, 'but he couldn't be left in a rubbish tip, could he?'

'I guess not,' Holly said reluctantly. Goodness knows why she had sided with the man, but for some reason, she felt that justice had not been done.

'He was in quite a state, apparently,' Carol said. 'His beard, his hair, even his toenails, were filthy. That's where the name had come from, I suppose,' she said. 'They probably had to scrub him clean with carbolic too. He was talked about often amongst the social workers. A difficult case to get right.'

Carbolic usually came into the charity shop first thing in the morning, and although he and Carol had known one another in the past, neither of them behaved in any way that might indicate there had ever been a connection. Carol was pleasant enough, as they all were, and the strange man often brought them a packet of biscuits or at Christmas, a tin of sweets.

Carbolic didn't come in to see them that morning though. Perhaps, Holly wondered frivolously, he and Betty had run off together. But that lunchtime, after Betty's desertion, they were all a little out of sorts. Carol certainly seemed to be as wound up as a freshly coiled spring and had openly shouted at a customer for trying to lift something out from the window display without asking her first.

Thomas shuffled in with the bag he always pulled behind him. He had told Holly once, that it was for helping him cross the road. A thing on wheels, the sort you might put your light luggage in, to take for a short break. Although goodness knows how it helped him get across the street. Still, he was rarely seen without it.

'Well then?' he asked, clapping his hands and showing her and Tricia his gapped teeth. His nasal hair twitched with excitement. It wasn't unusual for conversations to start mid-way with

Thomas, so even accompanied by his darting eyes, and his obvious delight, they weren't unduly alarmed.

Tricia, who had more patience for individuals like Thomas, asked him what the news was.

'Haven't you heard then?' he almost yelled.

'Shh – you'll frighten the other customers, Thomas,' Tricia said. 'Now, what's the story because we have work to do.'

Thomas turned from the desk and began pacing back and forth. 'Pigs!' he said, cawing like some decrepit animal.

Neither Holly nor Tricia responded.

'Pigs! Police!' he shouted. 'All over the bottom of the town. You'll be wondering what they're after, I expect.' He looked from one of them to the other, but Holly had already run out of tolerance.

'Thomas,' she said calmly and quietly. 'We couldn't give a monkey's shit if you want to know. But you clearly want to tell us, so do so, and then beat it.'

'That, that, well, that one who was here,' he said stammering and flailing his arms, obviously discouraged. He banged his fist on the desk. 'Her who was here always. I don't know her name. The old one. The ugly one.'

At this, Holly had to suppress a guffaw.

He met her gaze obstinately though. 'Aye,' he continued. 'It's her they're saying. It was her time. Found down there by the railway. Blood everywhere.'

The garish, mismatched garments that surrounded Holly, seemed to suddenly pitch. She stood motionless, now unaware of the voices around her. Then, stumbling from Tricia, she pushed past. She made it just in time to vomit in the bathroom sink.

**11**

'Mrs Scott's dead,' Michelle said, her cheeks flushed with horrified enjoyment. 'I just heard from one of the patients. Hit by a train. Would you believe it?'

'The old woman? The one who tried to sneak through the other week and nab one of the doctors?' asked Julie. 'She was only just in here again, seeing Dr Moreland the day before, wasn't she? I remember her in her silly woollen hat and gloves.'

Michelle nodded. 'That's right. And I read the hospital letter that came in about her at the end of the week too. She wasn't well. Cancer. Perhaps that's why she jumped.'

Julie shook her head. 'Oh God, no,' the younger girl said. 'There would have to be a better way to end it than that, wouldn't there?'

'Well, you'd have thought, but who am I to say?' Michelle asked. 'It would have been quick, I guess.'

'Messy,' Julie said and wrinkled her nose. 'I wonder who found her. Must have been a dreadful thing to discover.'

'Dreadful,' Michelle agreed.

It seemed that, although Glainkirk was shocked by the news, few were unduly upset as they came into the GP's surgery that day. Whenever the topic was mentioned, it was done in hushed, dramatic tones. Everyone agreed that it was a terrible fate to befall an elderly lady, but no one dwelt on the thing for too long. Suicide was quite unsavoury.

∼

CATHY ARRIVED EARLY. She came in before her senior partner James, which wasn't unusual. Even Michelle was not at the front reception when she crossed behind the desk to collect her letters. She returned to her room, keen to get on. It was an hour until her first patient was due in, and she might get through some of the lab results at the very least to clear time for the letters later.

She worked solidly, looking up momentarily on hearing the back door bang. Footsteps sounded on the carpeted corridor outside, as her colleagues also began their day. She listened as next to her, the door opened, and the light was switched on, indicating that her partner James was in the building also. Still, Cathy continued working, refusing to look up from her screen until there was a tap at the door.

James looked around the corner. 'How was it?' he asked, smiling.

Cathy leaned back in her chair now realising from her aching shoulders how long she must have sat hunched. 'Oh James,' she sighed, and he laughed.

'That bad?'

'Not really, but I'm glad to be done with reunions for another five years. All OK with you?'

He came into the room and shut the door. Cathy looked at her partner quizzically. He was still to remove his jacket, as he always did when he was consulting, even on a chilly day, and Cathy saw that his suit was creased.

'Don't suppose you've heard about the accident overnight?' he asked. 'I expect the police will be in later. The lady we were discussing the other day.'

Cathy was confused. She and James had discussed half a dozen patients recently, so he could have meant any one of them.

'Elizabeth Scott,' James said. 'Found dead this morning it seems. Talk of the town. The girls were telling me just now at reception. I assume the police will want a word. Looks like suicide. And given what you were saying about her diagnosis, there doesn't seem in any doubt as to why.'

Cathy was, for a moment, speechless.

'Elizabeth Scott's dead?' she finally repeated.

'Apparently so. They found her by the railway line just down from Fernibanks where she used to work. Absolutely tragic. But the police will no doubt fill us in. Thought I would give you the heads up. I assume she wasn't voicing any suicidal thoughts when you saw her last?'

'No. Not a thing,' Cathy said absently. 'James. I'm sorry, but I'm in shock.'

The senior doctor nodded. 'Nasty, I know, but presumably, there was nothing we could have done. Re-read her notes before the police come in. Familiarise yourself with it all. Cathy, don't start overthinking, OK? We can't spot everything, and if she didn't voice her desperation, then there really wasn't much we could have done. I know there's been enough violent death in Glainkirk to last us a lifetime, but suicides do happen.'

Cathy nodded. 'Thanks, James,' she said. 'Thanks for letting me know.'

James smiled. 'I'll leave you to it.'

Cathy felt sick. She couldn't believe it. Of course, they were wrong. The old woman hadn't killed herself; she was positive. She quickly opened Elizabeth Scott's notes, and read what she had herself typed the other day. She had documented the woman's refusal for treatment, and her own encouragement that she might change her mind at any point and that would be fine.

No, she decided. Betty Scott, for all of her eccentricities, was not of unsound mind though and certainly hadn't hinted at suicide. But she *had* voiced a real concern at the end of the consultation. Something serious had been troubling her. Something in Glainkirk, she had said. She had even gone as far as to say that it was someone in the charity shop who had made her feel edgy. Cathy tried to think of the old woman's words. Something to do with having been a psychiatric nurse and knowing when something was wrong. What had she meant? Had she been implying that she could spot when someone was becoming mentally unstable? Having worked as a matron up at Fernibanks, it seemed quite plausible. Cathy thought again of their last encounter. She pictured the fluffy, white-haired woman. She had been close to tears at one point, Cathy recalled. There was an air of desperation about her plea for help. 'Promise me,' she had begged. But of course, Cathy hadn't known what she was promising to do. She had been as reassuring as she could but had assumed that the old woman was exaggerating, or at least, she had hoped it was the case. Betty Scott had said that she was going to speak to the person in question first. If it didn't go to plan and they wouldn't agree to the old woman's demands, she was going to get Cathy to help. Was it possible that she had done just as she had said she would? Was it melodramatic to consider then that the encounter had resulted in her death?

Come afternoon, when the police did arrive at her door, Cathy had prepared an account of her patient's last couple of consultations. But more importantly, she told them about Mrs Scott's concerns about something, or rather someone, in the charity shop. The policeman, a detective whom she had dealt with over an assault case some months ago, smiled.

'I'll be honest,' he said. 'We will, of course, go and talk to the other volunteers at the shop, but it seems reasonably straightforward. Especially, given what you have told us about the breast cancer and likelihood of her dying in the next couple of months.'

'I know it sounds ridiculous,' Cathy said helplessly, 'but I got the feeling that she knew there was danger. I had assumed, not for herself.' She sighed and flopped back in her chair. 'I'll leave it with you of course,' she said. 'I just have a horrible feeling that there's something more to this than suicide.'

## 12

It wasn't long past two o'clock when the police finally appeared at the charity shop. After Thomas had gone, Carol had considered shutting, but as Tricia said, nothing had yet been confirmed, and their source of information could hardly be considered reliable. Holly, now that she had recovered from her initial embarrassing upset, thought that this was a little unfair. She had known Thomas for near enough four months, and although he was as repugnant a man as could be imagined, it seemed he was almost bound to speak the truth. Holly thought it was part of his disability. It must have been some weight to bear throughout his life.

They all knew in their hearts, however, that the news was bad. Everyone worked away quietly that afternoon. Less of the usual nonsense could be heard coming from the kitchen where Neil and Alex sorted their trinkets and tat. Usually, the conversation was politics, with Neil typically pronouncing loudly on his theories and beliefs and Alex starting a sentence and then being interrupted halfway through. At times, in the past, Holly had found it quite amusing to listen. Instead of the customary highbrow theatre, however, the place was quite gloomy.

The Christmas decorations were all but gone. While Holly had been off, Carol had encouraged Tricia to come in and do a massive 'cull of stock,' as she called it. The shop looked quite bare. But there were still some bits to be tidied, and a number of the children's clothes to be sorted. Woollen jumpers with snowmen on the front, and baby-grows that looked like grotesque Santa suits. Goodness knows what became of it all.

Holly found the monotony of the work of little comfort that day. It was hard to believe that they were a member of staff down. Repeatedly, she caught herself frozen whilst folding some garment or other, unable to make sense of what Thomas had said. She thought about going through to the kitchen to talk to Alex and Neil, but couldn't bring herself to do it.

Carol and Tricia, were speaking in hushed tones out at the front. They had been huddled there for most of the afternoon. Holly could imagine the conversation without actually listening. Since the news of Betty's misfortune, a wave of melancholy had befallen everyone. She couldn't understand why the thing had hit her so hard. She had cared little for the old woman and had no reason to mourn. But then, they had had a connection of sorts. Holly wondered if her final chance to find out the truth was now gone. Elizabeth. She had read that name again last night, running her fingertips over the print. It had to be a coincidence though. All the same, she was sure that Betty had known a good deal. How much, would probably always remain a mystery.

Carol had taken over the till, and it was she who first spoke with the police when they came in. Both officers were male, the two of them dressed in Hi-Viz, yellow jackets. Their radios crackled and squealed, disturbing the peace more than keeping it. They were unsurprised that the volunteers had already, albeit partially, heard the news. That was small-town gossip for you, and no secret was safe for long. The police finally confirmed their fears. Betty had been discovered dead. There wasn't any great or gory description, not of the kind that Thomas had given anyway. From what they said though, death was unlikely to have been caused naturally.

'Trouble,' Neil said, poking his head out of the kitchen doorway after they had gone. 'Knew it would be. Didn't take them long to get down here and find us. Alex?' he called behind him, 'have you got an alibi sorted yet?'

Alex could be heard snorting from the kitchen.

Holly had to admire Neil's breezy deportment. He was quite something, given that a colleague had just been confirmed dead.

'Did they have any leads?' asked Neil, who it seemed, was now an expert not only on politics but police investigations.

'They didn't say,' replied Carol. 'Well, they'd hardly tell me anyway, would they?'

They closed the shop of course, then and there.

That evening, Holly sat alone watching the local news. The story made second-to-top-spot, which wasn't unexpected given the tragic nature of the event. A grave-looking police officer was interviewed briefly on television. He spoke about the current investigation being fast-paced. He urged anyone in the vicinity of the railway line by Fernibanks that previous evening, to come forward with information, no matter how small. Holly took this to mean that they had absolutely no idea what had happened that night. Why on earth the old woman had ended up down by the railway wandering about in front of trains, was anyone's guess. If he was asking for trivial information, she suspected he would get just that. No doubt Thomas would phone up having watched the appeal, and tell them about a fresh dog shit he had stepped in as he passed by.

Holly felt sickened and turned the thing off, preferring to sit in silence. She looked around her. Her decision to come here had been impulsive, just as many of her choices had been. The greatest had undoubtedly been when she told Mr Robinson that she had made a decision. But despite never mentioning an interest in the subject before, he hadn't seemed surprised. Having no help from home, her preparation had been eased a good deal by her chemistry teacher. He had coached her on how to write the application and primed her for the interviews. When she received a conditional offer, she had wanted to tell him first. He shook her hand. His grip was warm and strong. She had been quite determined after that. She didn't care about the taunts in the corridor anymore, or that she invariably ate her lunch alone. This was her ticket to freedom and finding people like her. Her 'tribe'. When she passed with straight A's, she thought it was the proudest moment of her life. She looked down now at the scatter of papers and textbooks. She'd thrown it all away. Her one chance. What a waste. She'd let so many people down. Why had she brought all of this with her anyway? It was over. It was done.

Holly slept like the dead that night, but only after drinking herself into a near-stupor. She woke the following morning with her phone ringing, and when she answered, her heart sank further. It was Carol. The police were questioning all of the volunteers and she needed to be at the shop by ten.

As it turned out, the police weren't there, despite Holly arriving a good half-hour late. The rest of the volunteers were waiting though. Carol had busied herself and was lining up the least offensive mugs in the kitchen. It was Alex who was sent out front to open the door for her when she knocked.

'Not late, am I?' Holly asked hopefully, and Alex, to whom she had not in the past perhaps given enough time, grinned and told her that Carol was having kittens.

They walked together through to the back. The shop was

only dimly lit from the light in the kitchen, which shone a path through the shadowy mannequins and clothes rails.

'Carol doesn't want to attract customers,' Alex explained.

As they entered the kitchen, Carol turned from the kettle. Holly wondered if she was about to do her fainting trick again because she looked pale and haggard. Probably anaemic or something, she considered.

'Thank God for that,' Carol said dramatically.

Holly exchanged a look with Alex, her new conspirator.

'That's everyone then,' Carol said. 'I think it should all be straightforward enough. No need for anyone to worry and if there's a question you don't know the answer to ...'

'Miss it out and come back to it at the end of the exam,' Holly quipped. Neil and Alex guffawed, but Carol looked as po-faced as ever. Tricia, who held a dishcloth, wrung it enthusiastically, presumably wishing it was Holly's neck. Holly smiled jovially at Carol.

'You're not going to say silly things,' Carol stated.

'Am I not?' Holly asked. Her head was thumping with a hangover, but she wasn't going to show weakness in front of any of them.

It felt as if there had been a shift in dynamic since Betty had died. Carol's repeated attempts to take control of the situation had fallen flat. The so-called manager ran a forefinger over the line of her eyebrow. Back and forth once, then twice, and catching herself, she dropped her hand by her side as if she knew she'd been seen.

'Did you watch the news last night?' Holly asked the room.

Both Neil and Alex said that they had.

'Feels just like all those years ago. It's happening all over again,' Neil said, now comfortable in his self-appointed position of criminal expert having witnessed a violent death before, albeit a bloody lifetime ago. Holly couldn't abide the man and his supercilious demeanour, so she turned away. She was sure that Alex had noticed.

Having automatically made up everyone's usuals, Carol and Tricia began to hand around the mugs.

'Should we wait?' asked Tricia.

'What for? It's not as if we're sitting down to a slap-up meal with the police,' Neil said. Holly wondered if he was beginning to tire of the damn place as much as her. He raised his mug and the coffee slopped high up the side, spilling over slightly. 'Cheers. To Betty, God rest her soul,' he said. He pretended that his hand hadn't been scalded by the hot liquid, but Holly watched him for a minute and saw him rub it on his horrible corduroys, and then look at the side of his finger.

There was a definite sense of unease as they sipped their drinks, each one of them listening for the knock on the front door. Neil couldn't help himself. He was born to fill awkward silences and he fell back onto his rehearsed witticism once again.

'How're everyone's alibis looking then?' he said, placing his mug now on the wooden counter. No one answered, but Tricia smiled out of loyalty. Neil wasn't put off though. Presumably, he had lived a lifetime, making wise-cracks only to have them fall flat like cowpats.

'You got a good story?' he said, turning to Holly probably having spotted that she was out on a limb and not part of Carol's inner circle.

'I have no defence whatsoever,' she said. 'If they try to pin it on me, I can't argue. I was at home all night, but with nobody to corroborate my story, I can't prove a thing. I, though, had no reason to wish ill of Betty,' she said.

'What, and you're saying anyone else might?' Tricia suddenly said.

Holly turned to face her, taken aback. 'No Tricia, I think you know I wasn't saying that. I didn't think foul play was suspected at all, but you know what they say about a guilty conscience ...' she left it hanging.

Tricia didn't disappoint, throwing the dishcloth down on the sink top and pushing past Neil and Alex who had blocked the doorway. Poor Alex had been mid-sip, and as she flounced from the room, she jogged his arm and caused him to leap back away from the hot liquid. The coffee landed with a splash on the floor.

'We'll all be in A and E at this rate with third-degree burns,' Holly laughed.

The police arrived forty minutes later than they were meant to. By that time, Neil had become even more blasé, but Tricia was pacing the room and was clearly dying to get the whole interview palaver over and done with. Holly's stomach had taken on the hollow ache well-known to all who have ever over-indulged in alcohol. Fearing that her blood sugars were dropping too rapidly, she took a couple of biscuits from the tin and ate them meditatively while the policemen introduced themselves.

It was two officers once again, but this pair appeared more like high-flying businessmen, in relaxed but expensive suits. A whiff of masculine aftershave caught at Holly's throat as they entered the room, and she had to force the residue of biscuit crumbs over her gullet in a painful gulp. From their accents, it was clear that they were not from these parts. Holly thought that they must have been called in especially. Perhaps the local plod wasn't up to the job.

The senior detective introduced himself first, and then his colleague. He apologised for their delay. There was a murmur of understanding from Carol and Tricia, something Holly found detestably hypocritical given that five minutes before, the two women had been cursing their tardiness.

It seemed that they wanted to talk to anyone who had been working on the day that Betty had died, who might presumably have spoken with her in the shop and heard something indicating her state of mind. To Holly, this sounded a little far-fetched, but she supposed that they had to tick their boxes.

'Do you think she jumped then?' she asked when the detective had stopped the preliminaries.

The policeman closest to her turned. 'We're not making any assumptions. The postmortem will tell us more, but that is one definite line of inquiry.'

Holly thought that it was all rather odd. An old woman would hardly choose to die that way. She remembered Betty's hospital visits and wondered if the police knew something more. Had Betty been suffering from some incurable illness? Might this have been a motive to jump? Still, Holly thought it highly unlikely.

Carol had arranged some chairs and the fan heater in the back room. This was where they planned to speak to the volunteers in turn. Holly supposed that if any of them looked suspicious, they might take them down the station for a beating, or harsh questioning, or whatever form of interrogation the police force employed these days.

She was first up, not that she minded. They sat facing one another, all friendly and civil, with no mention of thumbscrews or waterboards. Holly's hangover was now long-forgotten. She rested back in the chair, determined to enjoy what was to come. They took down her name and address. She made a couple of gags about the weather or something. She told them from the start that she couldn't help them, that she was meant to have been passing through this God-forsaken town herself, but had ended up staying on longer. The senior detective, who she thought was called David, nodded as if he completely agreed with this sentiment. They asked about the charity shop, and Holly told them that she wasn't in paid employment currently due to ill-health, but that she had wanted to remain active and to give back something to the community whilst she was off sick. This little line pleased her a good deal, and she reminisced about it all that afternoon, chuckling to herself. There wasn't an awful lot more to say. Holly told them that she knew nothing of Betty's circumstances and what with Betty being far older, they naturally hadn't conversed much in the shop.

'So, have you got any real idea as to what happened?' Holly asked as the men shifted, apparently close to ending the interview.

'We're keeping an open mind. It's very early days,' the man David said.

'Do you think someone else might have been involved? Is that why you're asking questions?'

'It's unlikely, but certainly a possibility,' he said.

'Like an enemy?' Holly asked. 'I don't understand though,' she went on. 'Why would she go down there? She can't have been dragged to the railway. Someone would have seen, and if you're thinking she killed herself, why choose that horrible way to die?'

David looked a little miffed, and Holly sensed that the air grew slightly frostier despite the fan heater blasting away in their faces.

'No preconceived ideas,' he said shortly. 'We haven't found any CCTV yet to trace her movements. Unfortunately, the town has few security cameras in operation, and certainly none down the end where they might have been useful. We're speaking door-to-door but …'

He didn't need to say any more. Holly understood. The neighbours were all of a similar age and highly unlikely to have seen or heard anything of any use. Even if they had, they would make appalling witnesses.

'Would it have been quick?' Holly asked, turning back as she reached the door.

'Very,' the detective answered.

Holly nodded. It was a little solace, all the same.

•

## 13

Having hung around waiting to be dismissed following the interviews, Holly couldn't simply go back to her flat and stew. After what they had told her about Betty's end being so abrupt and brutal, she needed to be outside, and oddly, she wanted to be close to Betty. It was just past lunchtime but she had no appetite. The streets were crowded with shoppers, who despite the inevitable overindulgence over Christmas, seemed determined to adhere to a routine and buy their usual steak pie for a Thursday evening meal, or sausage roll for lunch at the butchers.

As she walked past the enormous glass window, she happened to glance in and see the man, white-coated and capped, raising his cleaver to some unknown meat. He hacked at it expertly, cutting it into more manageable portions. It was pink and glistening, and as he cut, he revealed a blushing inner.

Holly thought of poor, withered Betty, and with almost immediate self-disgust, pondered if she had looked the same. Holly wondered if the old woman had been complicit in her death. Had the end been swift, or had she been afraid? Had she cried out, or been still? Holly shook her head and plunged her hands deep into her pockets.

The bottom end of the high street was gridlocked. A delivery driver was attempting a three-point-turn in too narrow a space. The exhaust vapours billowed and clouded in the cool winter air. She had already noticed that some of the cars that had been parked there overnight still had white windscreens.

The delivery driver finally made a good job of it but received an indignant toot from the car first in line. A neighbouring pedestrian, who had been walking the other way, and now parallel with her, jumped in exaggerated alarm. It was only then, that Holly realised that it was Thomas, the man with a learning disability who had broken the news of Betty's demise.

His figure was stooped, like that of a far older person, with his jacket hanging loose and dishevelled around his shoulders.

'Aye, aye,' he said, which to be fair, was his customary greeting.

'Thomas,' she said. 'What are you up to then?' She didn't say it in an accusatory tone at all, but being as literally-minded as he was, he took it to be so.

'Nothing. I'm allowed to be here, aren't I? Just walking about. The police aren't after me. I've been in for my breakfast at Shirley's.' (This was one of the local teashops in town.) 'And I was coming down to see if you were open.'

'Obviously, we're not. How could we be after what's happened?' Holly said rather unkindly.

Thomas shrugged, and she knew she had worried him because he began running the zip to his jacket up and down, as he always did when he was anxious. She felt a pang of remorse.

'I'm just wandering,' she confessed. 'I'm a bit lost today. I was going to head down to Betty's.'

'Oh, I'll come. I was only on the lookout for numbers today anyway,' he said obscurely, and feeling as if she had been coerced into the situation through her own penitence, they set off together.

'Police been questioning you, then?' Thomas asked.

Holly was acutely aware of his bag, which he insisted on dragging behind him. It made the most awful noise as he scraped it along the ground.

'Yes. They've spoken to all of us. I don't think they're much further forward though. They were talking about it being suicide, but I can't see how it could be.'

'Marie doesn't think that,' Thomas said. 'I was talking to her about it, and she would know too.'

'Oh?' Holly asked. 'How would she know?' She didn't even know who Marie was, to be honest, but her name had been mentioned by Thomas several times in the past when he had been in the shop, and she assumed that she was one of his fellow learning disabled friends or one of his carers.

'Well, she'd know because it's Marie,' he said. His breath was bitter, a mixture of tobacco and vinegar. She couldn't help but grimace.

By now, they were nearing the end of the high street and the turn leading up to Betty's cul-de-sac.

'Who called the police anyway, I wonder?' Holly said suddenly as they rounded the corner to the start to Betty's street.

'Marie. That's what I told you,' Thomas said with exasperation. Holly stood still and he continued ahead, trailing his horrible bag like an accessory limb.

'You didn't say that at all,' she told him.

He turned and grinned his awful, yellow assortment of pegs and hooks at her. 'Come on, we'll go in for a news with her. She'll have biscuits. She always has.'

Only then did Holly understand. Marie was, of course, Betty's neighbour. No doubt the police had already spoken with her, but perhaps she might have seen something unusual.

Marie opened the door almost before they were down her front path. She had obviously been watching from her window and must have seen the odd pairing trudging down her drive. Her house was similar to Betty's in external appearance, and Marie herself was not unlike the woman who had died. However, if Betty had possessed some of the spark and witticism that Holly suspected, Marie had no such thing, it seemed.

'Aye, aye,' Thomas called out enthusiastically before Marie could speak. He was clearly proud as punch of his acquaintance and couldn't wait to show her off.

The flurried, elderly woman waved, and as they drew closer, she called out. Her voice was a frail soprano. 'What, not again, Thomas? What's the matter with you today? You're at sixes and sevens, up and down this street, aren't you? Have you been hunting for numbers again?'

She obviously had a soft spot for the pathetic creature. Holly wondered if perhaps she had no children of her own, or none that came to visit anyway. Maybe she had taken him on, like some bedraggled stray.

'Aye,' he said again, and now that they were at the top of the drive, he stopped, abandoning his bag, presumably because he thought he was on safe ground. He clapped his hands together and rubbed them vigorously.

'You're not misbehaving again?' Marie asked, and then turning to Holly, she smiled. 'He's always up to mischief.'

'Any news?' Thomas asked her, ignoring this. 'Have they been back again then, the pigs?'

Marie's brow furrowed. 'I told you not to call them that, Thomas. They're doing ...'

'I know, I know. You're telling me off again, aren't you? But you know what I mean.' He twisted his head suddenly, jerking his neck, and then leapt sideways onto Marie's lawn as if something had just passed him unexpectedly. Holly couldn't see what had made him do it. Even having known Thomas, albeit superficially, for a good number of months, this behaviour was rather disconcerting.

'Eh?' he shouted, and then embarrassed, he returned to normal, well as normal as he ever was. 'No nothing,' he said, 'I was just thinking about something.'

It was like some kind of slapstick comedy sketch. Holly was feeling more than a little awkward what with all of his dramatics going on. Standing right at the door of a stranger, she felt that she really should say something.

'Thomas said you alerted the police?' she decided on, and then to Marie's slightly dubious reaction, she explained: 'I work at the charity shop.'

'Of course, you do. I thought I knew your face.'

Holly didn't much like this, to be fair. She counted herself as pretty non-descript in appearance, and whenever she felt that she was beginning to be accepted as part of a group or community, she became twitchy and ended up doing something to ostracise herself.

'So, you've had a rather eventful couple of days,' Holly said, hoping to move things back on track.

Thomas was pacing up and down the lawn now and exaggeratedly sniffing the air. Both Marie and she ignored him. A ginger and white cat came wandering over and joined them. The animal came right up to Marie and the old woman bent down and picked it up.

'Betty's,' she said in explanation. 'But he always preferred it over at mine anyway, didn't you, 'Marmalade?' I've been feeding him for years,' she chuckled. 'Poor old Betty. Doted on her cat. Dreadful, the whole thing, and you'll be upset yourself having worked alongside her, I imagine. And so unexpected, especially in this town. Who would have thought that we harboured a murderer?'

'Oh, do you think that there was foul play?' Holly asked, surprised. 'The police said they still weren't sure and they were doing a postmortem. They've just been in questioning all of us.'

The cat was scrabbling to get down, and Marie leaned forward, allowing him to jump to the ground. 'It wasn't suicide. That I'm sure of,' she said.

'Thomas said it was you who called the police. He was the one who came in right at the start and told us at the shop, as it happens. That was the first we heard of it,' Holly said.

Marie shook her head and tutted. 'He's not good at keeping things to himself,' she said. 'Betty and I weren't close by any means. But I'd never wish ill of her. I was concerned, you see? First thing in the morning. She was always up, you understand? But the curtains, well, the top ones hadn't been pulled shut at all. I noticed when I did my own the night before. I thought it was odd. But then I thought she might be staying up to watch something on the television. That new period drama nonsense was starting, I seem to remember, and I think I must have wondered if it was the sort of thing she might watch. Not my taste at all,' Marie said, 'and on far too late to bother with anyway.' She smiled as Thomas now planted himself down on the grass, his legs cocked out oddly at the wrong angle. 'Comfy there?' she asked him, and then turning to Holly; 'he'll catch his death sitting on that cold ground, but he'll not listen. Do you want to come in? I've got biscuits.' At this, Holly almost laughed because Thomas evidently overheard and began getting up.

'I'll leave my bag outside,' he said reassuringly and marched in past them.

That settled it, and Holly followed, along with the ginger and white cat.

Marie had chosen pink as her main colour scheme and had bought near enough every damn thing in a rose-hue. It made Holly feel nauseous. The old dear fussed around getting the biscuit box to keep Thomas quiet, and he established himself at the far end of the room on, clearly, a favourite stool.

'Do you like her?' he asked in an audible whisper and nodded towards Marie.

Holly smiled. This seemed to satisfied him, and he sat almost entirely silent for the rest of their visit, munching his way through an assortment of custard creams, digestives and rich tea biscuits. Holly waived the proffered box, having seen the state of Thomas's hands. She didn't want to consume anything he might have picked up and rejected.

Marie sat down. She leant forward, making herself gasp with the exertion, and flicked a switch on her heater. The bar illuminated within seconds, a glow of fierce orange.

'Yes, so as I was saying,' the old lady said. 'I knew the night before, and I'll forever regret not doing anything. Poor Betty had lain like that all night alone. Who knows, if I had called someone, they might have been able to save her.'

'I don't think ...' Holly started.

'No, but you never know,' Marie said briskly as if to silence any commiseration. 'But the next morning, the curtains were still all wrong, so I went over. The door was pulled shut though. They lock, you know if you pull them from the outside. I've done it a couple of times myself by accident.'

Holly nodded, not wanting to interrupt again.

'So, knowing it wasn't right, I phoned, then and there, and of course, you know the rest. Sirens, blue lights, people running about. Dreadful.'

'Dead,' Thomas stated unfeelingly from the corner of the room, spitting biscuit crumbs across the carpet.

'Quite,' Marie said, her lips tightly pursed. 'It didn't take them long to find her. A man walking his dog ... Dreadful.'

'I didn't know Betty that well, as a person,' Holly said. 'She didn't talk that much in the shop ...'

'You're wondering who would do such a thing and why, I'm guessing?' Marie said, clearly far sharper than Holly had given her credit.

Holly was surprised that the woman was so convinced it was murder.

'Well, I don't want to speak ill, but she wasn't the easiest of women, and that's not a lie. Difficult, I'd say, and there'll be a few around these parts who won't miss her. I've not said this to the police of course,' Marie said, shaking her white, fluffed head. 'They'd not want to hear that. No. But a few folks have already been saying it, up and down the town, but that's just gossip, you see? No, but what I can tell you for sure is that Betty's act of doddering old lady, well, it wasn't Betty at all. I've seen first-hand how ruthless she could be. I suppose it came with the job, back in the day.'

To Holly's raised eyebrows, Marie explained.

'Matron, and a pretty fearsome one too by all accounts. Up at the old hospital,' she went on. 'Fernibanks. Betty was the matron of the psychiatric hospital. There's a good few who'd not mind her gone. It's a wonder it's taken so long. Murder though, and right on our doorsteps too.'

## 14

Cathy sat in her consulting room and worried. She felt a great weight of responsibility given that it was she who Betty Scott had chosen to confide in. The more she thought about it, the more convinced she was that it wasn't suicide, no matter what the police said. Already, they had dismissed her suggestion of foul play as fanciful. She had been made to feel foolish. She could only hope that the postmortem might reveal something. But what was she meant to do while the police waited, dragging their heels? Could they assume it was suicide? Cathy thought again of the old woman's look of anguish when they last spoke. Her imploring eyes. 'Promise me ...'

'Oh God,' Cathy sighed. 'Well, promise you what, Betty? I don't even know what you meant.' If only the old woman had said more.

Impulsively, she snatched up the telephone. The police officer who had visited the other day had left his card in case she needed to get in touch with him again and she quickly dialled an outside line and waited.

She didn't manage to speak to the same man, but instead, a colleague who was at first sympathetic to her concerns, and then increasingly patronising. 'Yes, Doctor,' he had said. 'I'll be sure to make him aware of your concerns just as soon as he gets back. No, of course, I understand that you get a gut-feeling about these things in your line of work. I suppose we're similar in that respect. No, if you've already told him about your consultation with the old lady, I doubt he'll need to speak in-depth again, for now, that's unless something else comes up. I can promise you that we're very busy making inquiries. Looks very likely that she jumped, poor soul. No, no need, if he has your number. I'll let him know ...'

Cathy had replaced the receiver feeling more frustrated still. Well, how was she to get on with things, knowing that she had been Betty's sole confidant? The old woman had had something on her mind, something of grave importance. If only she hadn't been so determined to speak with the other person first.

'Alright, Dr Moreland?' Michelle had asked as she passed her door later that morning.

'Oh, just a bit distracted,' Cathy confessed, taking the prescription the receptionist held out and signing it absent-mindedly.

'About your old lady?' Michelle asked. 'Talking about her with Dr Longmuir earlier. Unbelievable really. I saw the police had been in.'

'Yes. I spoke on the phone with them again just now. That's what's troubling me.'

'You're surely not blaming yourself though. But you couldn't have known,' Michelle said. 'My second-cousin did away with himself. Auntie Yvonne didn't have an inkling. These things happen, I suppose, and if she was dying anyway ...'

Cathy looked at the young woman. 'That's just it, Michelle. Things like this *don't* just happen. Not to an elderly woman. Not when she was dying. No one would choose that way to die. No one.'

Michelle took the paper and shrugged. 'Will I leave your door ajar?'

But Cathy didn't answer.

It wasn't right. None of it. The police were wrong. They were too quick to dismiss it as suicide and if they weren't taking the thing seriously, Cathy wondered what might be missed during the investigation. Had they even looked at the scene of the crime? In their acceptance of it being a simple death, were they missing half a dozen incriminating clues left behind by the murderer?

Well, she was the duty doctor for the day and had a couple of visits to do. One was on that side of Glainkirk. She might easily park up, and take a look for herself. She had every right to do so.

It was a cool morning, and still overcast. Having seen to her visits and checked back with the practice that no others had come in, Cathy parked her car down a side-street near the railway line. Here, she considered the task at hand. She had half expected to see some form of a police presence, at least some blue-and-white tape indicating that they had been in attendance, but there was nothing to show that the area had been witness to a gruesome disturbance the day before.

Although it was mid-morning, there wasn't a soul in sight. The doctor, unsure of quite where to begin, stepped off the road and onto the grassy bank that edged the railway lines. She wore fur-lined, leather ankle-boots, which was as well, given that the grass was long and damp. In parts, the railway was fenced with sagging barbed wire and the posts, which should have supported this, were rotten and at odd angles. It was hardly surprising that there had been an accident. Although of course, this had not been an accident at all, and she had to find any evidence to prove it. Poor Betty Scott had taken her last breath just here. Cathy paused for a moment and thought of the elderly woman, so ill, and yet so robust and full of character and determination. What a sad end.

She began to step carefully as she looked. She didn't quite know what she expected to find, but even if the police had tramped back and forth a dozen times recovering Betty's body, she still felt the exercise worthwhile, even if it was only for her peace of mind.

She came to an area on the verge where it was obvious that a car, if not several, had been stationed. The tyre marks dug deep into the damp ground, and it seemed that the wheels had spun, spraying mud onto the long grass. This, she assumed, must have been where the police had parked. She followed a quite obvious path of flattened grass down to the stony railway siding. Was this the spot? She shivered thinking of the awful discovery and looked up and down the line, in case a train might be approaching. She had no intention of crossing or going anywhere near the rails though.

Cathy felt it unlikely that the police would have missed anything, but given their lackadaisical approach so far, she felt she should check to be sure. She leaned down and spent some time hunting amongst the flattened grass for anything of note. A good many footprints were visible from people tramping up and down the area. The track was quite muddied in places. For completeness, Cathy continued up the line. Carefully, she stepped over the already collapsed fencing. She looked along the road and saw that if she continued this way, the one parallel with the railway would meet the next side-street. She thought it was Broad Street. If Betty had approached the railway from further up, there might still be something to find there.

Her monotonous work continued. Several times, she paused, seeing litter in amongst the grassy verge, and considered if it might be relevant. It was hard to tell if anyone had walked this way as the ground was quite packed down. Eventually though, nearing the junction that would take her directly in line with Broad Street, and some fifty yards from where the body must have been found, she stopped to consider the undergrowth by the pavement. Here she saw that the grasses had been flattened in a well-demarcated manner. It seemed that the patch of scrubland was compressed in an almost perfect rectangle, the size perhaps of a small suitcase if it had lain on its side. Cathy knelt and touched the grass. A weight had undoubtedly lain there, but the grass was not so indented as to affect the soil beneath, meaning that the object had not been unduly heavy.

Cathy continued to scan the area. She hoped to find some fluff from Betty's hat or gloves or something equally tangible, but she was disappointed. There was no further trace of the old woman. Opposite Broad Street itself, it seemed that the fence bordering the line was almost flat. Cathy thought that perhaps here might be the easiest place for a person to cross if they had wanted to. Was this the site where Betty Scott had passed on foot? Had the old woman then walked parallel to the line, to finish at her final resting place further along, and if so, why? There certainly appeared to be the general appearance of the admittedly short grass, lying at a flatter angle than the rest.

Standing up once more, Cathy quickly checked her phone in case the surgery had tried to call. No call had come through. As she looked about her, she considered the desolate spot. A dumping ground for litter, and even garden waste. Up above the line, the old psychiatric hospital sat, eerily empty. But what stories might it have told, had the broken and boarded up windows been able to speak? What a dreadful place to die. If she had had her way, Betty Scott would have lived out her time in comfort. Her final days spent in a warm, safe place, not here in some muddy tip, cold and afraid.

Cathy sighed. She was beginning to feel cold herself. Still looking carefully this way and that, in case she had missed something, then slowly made her way back in the direction of her car. In a way, she didn't want to look out onto the railway lines themselves, but she cast her gaze across the pebbles, knowing that if she did not, she might potentially miss something important. Now in line with the tyre tracks again and where the body must surely have been found, she paused again, seeing some of the leaves had been disturbed. She crouched down and peeled back the damp vegetation. Beneath a fallen leaf, perhaps not more than a few drops, was unmistakably blood.

Cathy was well accustomed to trauma and death. Nevertheless, she could not repress the feeling of revulsion as she contemplated this discovery. Betty Scott, a woman already dying from cancer, but a person full of vigour, and with purpose in her charitable work, had been killed. Of that, she was sure. She had spoken to the old lady on more than one occasion and had admired her determined manner. Had she not known of Betty's concerns; the doctor would have said that she was the last person on earth to be murdered. Why kill someone who was going to die in the next couple of months, anyway? Considering the desolate spot for the last time before getting into her car, Cathy exhaled. It was sickening to imagine the old woman being led or forced down to the railway line that evening, let alone, being thrown in front of an oncoming train. She felt sure that if it was so, there was someone in Glainkirk of such evil, that it was beyond her comprehension.

## 15

Holly got the impression that Marie felt embarrassed or guilty about what she had said about Betty. She became restless having divulged that the old woman was universally disliked, and it was so palpable that Holly felt she should leave. She wanted to ask her, there and then, all about Betty and exactly what Marie had meant. But she thought it better to wait. There would be other people who would talk, there had to be if, as Marie said, there had been gossip going around.

Thomas left with her. He completely omitted to express any thanks for the biscuits and appeared almost indifferent towards poor Marie, who seemed to dote on him all the same.

'Keep out of bother,' the old lady called after him, and he turned and grinned.

'You mean away from him, don't you? She knows about him,' he said, pointing towards Holly.

Marie shook her head and smiled.

'Who?' Holly asked as they walked down the drive. 'Who are you talking about now?'

'You know. You know. Him. Carbolic. Trouble, but don't you

be telling him I said it. You'll not, will you? He'd probably come at me and push me in front of a train, wouldn't he? Do you think he might? What if he comes to my door tonight with a knife and makes me walk down there?'

'Don't be ridiculous,' Holly said, but it put an idea in her mind all the same. 'Where are you heading now?' she asked as they continued up the cul-de-sac.

'Nowhere. I'm following you, aren't I?'

Holly shrugged. She felt rather shaken by Marie's assumption that Betty had been murdered. In truth, she had suspected something as soon as the old woman had failed to arrive at work that previous morning, but things had escalated so rapidly since then. For the first time since arriving in Glainkirk, Holly felt quite out of her depth.

'I'm heading back uptown again,' she said definitely.

'I'm coming,' Thomas told her, and she was glad.

'One, two, three, four. Carbolic, carbolic,' Thomas chanted as they set off. 'You'll be thinking it's him that's done it, maybe. Carbolic. Imagine if it was him. I'd like it if he went to prison.'

Holly didn't answer. She was imagining poor old Betty being frog-marched down to the railway line in the damp, cold of the evening, perhaps with a knife to her back. Being held until the lines began to sing and the train was almost upon them. The lights would have been blinding. Had she fought, or was she so afraid that she had stubbled backwards and into the path of the engine?

It seemed that the high street was still reasonably busy. The cars had their lights on dipped-beam, and the sound of their tyres as they passed, made a satisfying swish. Holly found herself having to hang back at times to wait for her peculiar companion, as he shouted exclamations if anyone passed by too close. This, it seemed, disconcerted him, and on two occasions he performed his bizarre manoeuvre, the one that she had seen on Marie's lawn, leaping sideways suddenly and clutching at his jacket.

'I wish you'd stop skipping around like that,' she said, not unfairly. His unpredictability was making her jumpy too, and she was jittery enough as it was.

'The people when they pass, keep making my ears itch,' Thomas said as if this was a reasonable explanation.

They arrived, still together, despite Thomas's attempts to get himself killed crossing the road by dodging in and out of the cars and then holding up his bag like some kind of a shield to protect himself. An oncoming red van was forced to brake suddenly and the driver threw his hands up in exaggerated despair.

She found herself sitting in Shirley's, the café across the road from the charity shop, barely knowing how they had got there in one piece. Thomas sat down opposite and ordered his usual, whatever that meant, and Holly asked for a pot of tea and thought about her discoveries. Betty had been linked to Fernibanks. Was she the Elizabeth she was searching for? Perhaps she had been right all along.

'What do you think then?' Thomas asked after she had sat gazing despondently out of the window for some time.

'About Betty? I don't know Thomas. Honestly, I don't know what to think anymore. I came here for something different and now I'm in the midst of all this.'

'Eh? What do you mean something different? Did you want a scone or a buttery?'

Holly looked back at his open, expectant face, but the girl brought over his usual, which appeared to be an all-day breakfast, and he was lost to anyone after that. She sat sipping her tea, trying to ignore the harrowing noises coming from across the table. Never before had she seen anyone eat with such a ferocious enjoyment.

'Don't you bother much with cutlery then?' she asked at one point, and he opened his mouth wide, tipping his head back and laughed, displaying a semi-masticated piece of bread.

'Aye, Aye, I'll not bother then today,' he said, spitting toasty crumbs across the table at her and clapping his sticky hands in gleeful delight.

'Disgusting,' she said, but part of her rather enjoyed his all-encompassing pleasure in such a simple thing as beans, sausages, eggs and toast.

The staff were used to this display and watched their table in amusement.

'Wonder if she had a time too,' Thomas said as he mopped up the tomatoey sauce on his plate with a bit of toast. 'They all do, you know? I expect I'll get one soon. I'm looking out all the time for my own time to die. It's tricky though. Numbers everywhere.' This sent him off into a fit of chuckling and coughing once more.

'Does everyone know you in this town, Thomas?' Holly asked after he had placed his napkin down on the plate at last, sitting back and sighing.

'Aye. I expect they do.' He laughed again. 'Aye, they'll probably all know me.'

'Haven't you got any family then?'

'Nope. Mother died, or was ill when I was a baby.'

'And your father?'

'I didn't have one of them,' he said simply.

'Well, you must've had a father, Thomas. Who brought you up?'

'Oh, I don't know. Folks here and there.'

Holly nodded and suddenly felt a lump in her throat.

'I need to go,' she told him, hurriedly pushing back her chair and allowing its feet to screech in protest. He looked up; his lips still moist with tomato sauce. Although she hated to say it, his clear disappointment, tugged at her heart-strings.

'I'll come in again and see you at the shop,' he said, but she wasn't sure when they would next open.

Holly walked the dank street, thinking of her father; someone who had always been there, but who she hadn't noticed until he was gone. The crematorium had been packed. A popular man. Well-known and well-liked. Simple and unassuming. What would he think of her choices if he was still here? Not a lot, she assumed. She should be at home consoling her grief-stricken mother, not here, on a self-seeking bender.

'It's understandable for you to be upset,' her mother had said on the evening of the funeral. 'The university won't expect you back for a few weeks surely. I know your studies are important to you, but some time to get over things is what you need.'

Holly had been sitting at the kitchen table with a whisky glass held defiantly in her hand. Most of the extended family had returned home now and the silence was deafening.

'It'll only numb you for a few hours,' her mother pleaded. 'Why not have a cup of tea with me and your aunt instead before she heads home? What would Dad say about this?' she said, half-laughing and pointed to the bottle on the table. 'He'd give you a real telling off, wouldn't he?' Her voice wavered and Holly clenched her teeth, hating herself. But her mother had lied. They all had.

She swilled the liquid in the glass.

'I wish you'd talk to me,' her mother went on.

Without speaking, Holly reached into her back pocket and withdrew the papers she had found. Slowly, she unfolded them and laid them there flat.

She didn't see her mother's reaction. She couldn't bear to look at her then. downing the glass-full of amber liquid in one swift movement, she got up. She'd always hated whisky and now it would remind her of that night forever.

God, what a mess. Her feet smacked on the wet pavement now, taking her back to the flat. She gazed down at her reflection in a muddy puddle, the wavering lights of the passing traffic highlighting her haunted features. Even unfortunate Thomas, for all of his strange mannerisms and ways, had found a place for himself.

She stopped at the off-licence. The brightly-lit sign, an almost neon-yellow, jaundiced the complexion of even the light drinker if they stood outside for long enough. Holly carried her bag of booty, the two bottles clinking together harmoniously as she went. She knew that the vodka would help. It always did. It not only numbed the past, but more recently, she had noticed it loosening the present and, if taken in the right measure, she hoped it might unwind her mind enough to think more clearly about the future.

In a moment of reckless impulse, Holly hovered at the end of her street wondering if she wanted to go back to the flat alone. It was now almost tea-time, and the commuters were winding their way home, preparing for cosy evenings in with loved ones, probably watching the second episode in a three-part drama together after the kids had gone off early to bed. Cuddling up on the sofa with a glass of wine and revolting companionable intimacy. Holly grimaced.

She knew where he lived. She knew where all of them lived, of course. There had been a recent change between her and Alex. She wondered if he had felt it also; the shared understanding almost, back in the charity shop when the police had been in. Why she had ignored the man up until then was beyond her. They were, after all, the only two of similar age. Well, perhaps he was a little under ten years her senior, at a guess, but compared to the rest of them, they were of the same generation at the very least. She had been too busy thinking of other things and hadn't noticed his affable, quiet way, and his harmless manner. Besides, he reminded her a little of her old chemistry teacher and surely that meant something.

By the time Holly had allowed her feet to take her to his door, she realised that she knew so little about Alex. She couldn't even be sure that he wasn't married. She started to get edgy and had half-decided to turn back for home, but in hovering by the porch, she had activated a movement-sensitive spotlight. Almost immediately, there was a twitch of one of the downstairs curtains.

Holly wasn't sure how he would react. She must look like some kind of a weirdo turning up at his door uninvited, clutching two, full, litre bottles of clear oblivion. But if he was surprised or shocked to see her, he didn't show it, and when he came to the door in his usual jeans and collared tee-shirt, there was no question about whether she would be invited in.

'Is it raining?' he asked, probably finding comfort in this safe topic. 'Here, let me take that.'

He hung up her jacket on the bannister after she had made a meal of removing it whilst still clutching the clinking parcel. This, she finally placed on the floor in the hallway, feeling too embarrassed to offer a bottle as a gift.

'Big night planned then?' he asked, grinning. He led her through to a comfortable sitting-room. The fire was lit and it burned a welcoming glow. The wood cracked and spat a cascade of luminous embers. Holly jumped at the noise and Alex laughed.

'I suppose we're all a bit like that just now,' he said.

'Alex,' she started, but wasn't quite sure what she was going to say. After all, how do you bring up the fact that you suspect a colleague of being murdered? But Alex was more comfortable at home than at work, and he had already brought through two glasses.

'Oh,' Holly said hesitantly. 'I didn't mean to stay Alex. I was just wanting to ask you something.'

She took the wine all the same, not that she liked the stuff very much. It would have been rude not to though, and together, rather awkwardly, they sipped.

It turned out that he was a bloody ex-police officer, didn't it? She could hardly believe it when he said, and after the first glass, he told her that he had been given early retirement due to ill-health. He rubbed his knee. 'Work-related,' he said, 'hence why they paid me off and why I can afford to bum around here and offer my time at the charity shop. Just to keep busy really. What about you?'

Holly got a little fidgety when he asked this, even though her speech was lubricated with the alcohol. 'Do you mind if I don't?' she asked, and he laughed and refilled her glass. In many ways, she marvelled at the transformation from mild-mannered, shy Alex to the man in front of her now.

'What do you think then?' she asked. The conversation had led them back to Betty as of course, it must. 'I just can't work it out, Alex. I have a strong suspicion that she was very ill indeed. Did you notice how thin she had become? I wondered about cancer. I've been trying to get my head around it. Even if she was unwell, I can't see suicide as being an option. I don't think the police believe that either. Why would an old woman choose that way to end it? An accident is just as bizarre. Why go down to the railway line in the evening at all and then inadvertently fall in front of a train? No. it has to have been murder. But who would care whether the old woman lived or died? It's not as if anyone benefited from her death, did they?'

Alex placed his glass on the table and leaned forward, resting his elbows on his knees. 'That's what you say, but you know it's not true. Oh, don't get me wrong, I haven't a clue about her financial situation. There might be a motive in that as well, for all we know. I'm only talking about the charity shop, but there are probably countless others too. She wasn't the nicest of people, in many ways. The way she spoke to Carol sometimes was outrageous. Even Neil and her were frosty. I only caught the tail-end of one conversation between them, but it had something to do with his old business, God knows what. He had a face like thunder when I walked in though.'

'How do you mean?' Holly asked, taking another swig of the wine. 'I suppose you'll be an expert in all this having been a policeman anyway.'

'Hardly.'

'Do you keep in touch with the people you worked with?' she asked.

'God no. I didn't want to leave in the first place, and what would I say to them now? Tell them I'm doing odd jobs for a few neighbours and working in a charity shop? No. That's a lifetime ago for me.'

She knew what he meant. It seemed that he too had a past that troubled him, perhaps they all had, in a way.

'I'll open another,' he said getting up. It appeared that between them they had worked their way through an entire bottle of wine. 'And you'll stay for tea? It's just pasta or we could push the boat out and order in.'

Holly got up, feeling surprisingly dizzy given that the actual units of alcohol she had consumed must have been reasonably low for her. 'No,' she said firmly. 'I think I'd better go. Otherwise, I might never leave.'

Alex raised his eyebrows, so she grabbed her jacket and bolted for the door with still so many questions unanswered.

'Does Neil know you were in the police?' Holly asked before

staggering her way down the greasy front path and winding her way home.

'I should walk you,' he said, making as if to get his jacket, but she was insistent and he eventually relented. 'No,' he said, 'I've not told anyone in the charity shop about my past. It's none of their business really.' And then, reaching out to her as she wobbled; 'you're sure you'll be alright?'

Holly threw him a carefree wave over her shoulder as she left. It wouldn't do to make two friends in the space of a day.

# 16

'They've made an arrest,' came Carol's breathless voice. 'I'm letting everyone know in case you hear it in the street. I didn't think that was fair on anyone. I had enough of a shock when I heard it myself. The postmortem showed that she was dead before the train hit her. She was murdered! She'd been hit on the head by someone first. I suppose it's a blessing in some ways but still ...'

It was gone half-two and Holly had only just returned home having purchased a fragrant and, frankly, slimy sausage roll from the butchers on the way past.

The crumbs of flaky pastry lay conspiratorially on the plate by the sink. As she moved across the kitchen with the phone to her ear, she paused and prodded at them, swirling the scraps around and around and then individually flicking them into the sink, watching as they landed at random and stuck to the damp metal surface. Ten points for the plug. But Carol interrupted the game.

'Did you hear me? An arrest,' she said again.

'Who was it then?' Holly asked impatiently. The silly woman probably didn't even know. She was phoning with half a story and expecting her to sit up and applaud like some fat sealion.

There was a pause. 'It's Thomas,' Carol finally said.

Holly froze. She nearly dropped the bloody phone in the sink.

'Thomas?' she repeated. 'What, Thomas, who comes into the shop? It can't be him. I was just talking to him.'

'That's who they say did it. Thomas. Apparently, they have evidence of some kind. Well, enough obviously to take him in for questioning anyway. I'm phoning around the others. I don't suppose you've seen –'

Holly hung up before Carol could say anymore. She was done with listening. They had got it wrong. Who in their right mind could imagine feckless, crazy Thomas having the ingenuity to pull off a murder? She couldn't imagine a less likely candidate if she tried. What were the police playing at, and what was it that they had on him anyway?

Holly grabbed her jacket from the hallway. Although she had only spent a relatively short time with the man, she knew it was all wrong. She could just visualise his panic-stricken face. He was such an innocent. She thought of his mad behaviour, of him leaping about at even the sound of a car horn, of him disliking the proximity of anyone if they stood too close. She knew that the police had procedures for dealing with people like him, they had to. There would be a responsible adult, or interpreter, or whatever they called them, to help him understand. Someone to explain the implications of the answers he gave them. But still, Holly felt that he would be like a fish out of water, and frightened. That was the worst of it really; imagining him sitting bewildered, not knowing what he had done wrong.

She slipped as she half-jogged her way down the close. The pavements were inky-black and patches that had not yet caught the sun were quite icy. As she neared the corner of the cul-de-sac, she slowed, afraid that she might fall on the tarmac. She assumed that Marie would be in and of course, she was correct.

'Have you heard?' Holly asked, breathlessly. Her fevered words met the cold air, turning them to vapour in front of her.

'I know, I know,' Marie said, 'Come in.'

She went in through the familiar hallway, and Marie led her back to the pink room in which the three of them had sat only the day before. There was no offer of biscuits or tea this time though. Holly looked at the stool in the corner, where he had munched his way through the best part of a packet of Rich Teas along with the rest, scattering crumbs with carefree abandon.

'I only just heard,' Holly told her, turning to look at Marie's worried face. 'How about you? Is it all around the town then?'

'He was here when they came. They kept saying it was just for formal questioning and not an official charge yet, but that's bad enough isn't it?'

Walking across to the chair by the fire, she lowered herself into it heavily. She landed awkwardly and winced, stretching a hand behind her back to adjust the rose velour cushion. She pulled the pillow out completely and sat with it on her lap, tracing patterns on the velvety fabric without knowing she did it.

'The police came here?' Holly asked, feeling as if she was sounding very stupid indeed. 'Did they give a reason? I just can't imagine them believing he had it in him. I mean, Thomas?'

Marie shook her head.

'I don't know much about the man, but you clearly do. Why do they think it was him?' Holly asked.

'They said they had found a patch of blood by the bins where he lives up at The Court,' she replied sighing. 'Apparently, it's being examined and tested, but they know already that it's human.'

'But that doesn't mean it was him. It could have been anyone. What about Carbolic? He lives at The Court too, and all of the rest of them. Tricia from the charity shop even goes in to visit some old dear up there as well. It could have been her, or any of the people who work there.'

'I know,' Marie answered.

'There has to be more,' Holly said defiantly. 'Had he and Betty even known one another? I know she saw him occasionally in the shop when he came in, but was there anything else?'

Marie looked uncomfortable. Eventually, when she spoke, her words came out in a heavy monotone, like she was reciting it without feeling. Her hands, by this time, had stopped moving and she clasped them as if had she not, they might escape.

'I never liked the woman, I told you that already,' she began. 'My husband used to call her 'The Ice Queen'. Seemed to hate men. Her poor husband didn't stay around for long. Certainly, she didn't stand for children running about the street making noise.' Marie sighed. 'You want to know about Thomas? He used to come down here regularly. I bumped into him quite literally in the street a good few years back now, not long after Arthur died.' She gestured to the mantlepiece and a gilt-framed photograph of her husband looked solemnly down. 'Well, you know yourself what Thomas is like. So naïve, and in a way, I suppose I felt rather sorry for him, as you do too.' She glanced across at Holly now, seeming to find her voice properly once more. She laughed and it sounded tuneful like a breeze playing on windchimes. 'He's quite a character, is Thomas. I think, what with losing Arthur, I was looking for something, maybe someone, and Thomas was there. We were almost fated to be friends. I needed him just as much as he needed me, you see? It was equal.'

Holly nodded.

'He used to come down here a lot at the beginning. I think that I must have been the first person in a long time to take an interest. I used to look forward to our funny little conversations.

He's far smarter than he makes out, you know? He has a wonderful memory for numbers and dates and times. Anyway, I suppose I must have encouraged him too much. He was quite a bit more boisterous than he is now.'

Holly laughed. 'He's bad enough now.'

Marie smiled. 'Well, believe me, he was a lot louder back then. Used to come down the street singing and calling out to me. Before he even came around the corner, he was shouting and carrying on. Sometimes if I was out, he told me he had waited on the doorstep. Every-so-often, he'd sit there, possibly for hours waiting until I got home, just so that he could have a news with me and a biscuit.'

Holly smiled at the thought of his silly figure, curled up on Marie's porch, rocking and singing until she returned.

'He had nobody really,' she said. 'I got onto the social services about it after a while and he now has these organised days out, and at least he's at The Court being looked after. But back then, he was like a lost child. Not a bad bone in his body. The social work people knew of him of course, but he had gone off the radar a bit. They're busy enough as it is.'

'Is it right then, that he has no one? He told me he had no family.'

'In a way, that's true. His mother, I believe was also mentally a bit not-there and easily swayed. I think poor Thomas may have been the product of a violent encounter. These sorts of things happened more frequently than you'd think, back in the day. His mother wouldn't have been able to care for him anyway, even if she had wanted to, and he was passed from pillar to post.'

'Is his mother still alive then?'

Marie shrugged her tiny shoulders. 'Who knows. She'd be no use to him now anyway.'

'So, I still don't understand why he'd have a motive to kill Betty.'

'No, I'm not explaining very well, am I?' The old lady smiled and then sighed. 'Betty took a dislike to Thomas. It was really intense and quite unjustified. She came over here on a couple of occasions complaining about the noise he was making when he came to visit, even said he was tormenting her cat or some such nonsense. She threatened to tell the RSPCA but as far as I knew he'd just been throwing stones for the poor creature to chase. You can imagine. You'd have thought in her line of work in the past, she'd have been more understanding, wouldn't you? But no. I told him to calm himself down a bit, but it only made him worse.' Marie twisted her hands in her lap. 'It came to a head at the end of last summer. He had been drinking. You know he does sometimes? He came down the cul-de-sac singing and shouting, and Betty came out of her house and had a real to-do with him in the street. Well, you know how that went, what with him being drunk and silly. Betty went back into her house, and how I wished I had known what he was about to do, but I didn't, you see?'

'What did he do?' Holly asked.

'It was so childish and I offered to pay, of course. There was no point in her going to the police and making a big fuss, but she wouldn't listen. He was cautioned at the time.' Marie looked at her now. 'He threw a brick in her front window,' she said.

Holly sat back in the chair. She blew a tuft of fringe off of her face. 'Now I understand,' she said, 'and so, they never really got on after that?'

'And me and her neither. There are ways of dealing with things, and she went about it the wrong way. Vindictive that was.'

Holly grimaced. 'She was murdered first. They say she was hit on the head. It wasn't the train that killed her at all. So, the police think that poor Thomas did it out of revenge of some sort. I take it he doesn't have an alibi for that evening?'

'He wasn't with me anyway,' Marie said. 'But of course, it wasn't him. They've just settled for the most obvious and vulnerable person, and it's wrong.'

'And if they have Thomas in custody, it means the killer's free and probably thinking that they're mighty smart for having pinned the crime on him.'

Holly left not long after that. Marie seemed glad that she had come and even suggested that she return if she heard any more news. Holly gave the old woman her mobile number just in case. Maybe Marie saw her as some kind of vigilante, and perhaps in a way, she was.

When Holly looked at her mobile as she walked home, she saw that she had three missed calls. All were from Carol. She was glad to have missed them, but Carol had left a message anyway. In it, she sounded irate, which made the corners of Holly's mouth prick for the first time that afternoon. Walking home, she felt even more determined. Carol had said that the shop was opening again in the morning. They were all to come in. At least Holly would be doing something useful and she knew in her heart, that the answer to Betty's death was there, in amongst the shabby overcoats and random candlesticks.

## 17

'Crazy Thomas,' Michelle whispered.

'Unbelievable,' Julie mouthed. 'You never can tell with loonie folk though, can you? I'd never have put him down as one though, a murderer, I mean, would you?'

Michelle scrunched up her face. 'Mental age of a five-year-old or whatever. Something sent him over the edge, I guess. Maybe she looked like his dead mother who used to hit him or something. You read about things like that happening all the time. Something snaps and they go totally wild.'

Julie whistled quietly. 'My God. Well, I suppose it's as well he's behind bars now and not ranging around the streets. I used to see him all over the town, dragging that horrible bag behind him everywhere. Always crossed to the other side of the road when I saw him, and I'm glad I did now.'

'He's not been in to see any of the GPs for a while, has he? I think he was seeing the podiatrist every few months but I've not had to deal with him at all.'

'Me neither, thank goodness. It always comes out though, doesn't it? And it's usually the crazy ones that do it. I know it's not particularly politically correct. There'll be a big inquiry, I imagine.'

'Definitely, and the doctors'll be involved, no doubt. Having to give evidence about his character and whatnot, I imagine. Whether it could have been prevented in some way.'

'Oh well, we'll hear more later on. I'm just glad they caught him so quickly. And we had thought it was suicide too. Poor old Betty Scott. Murdered.'

∼

THOMAS HOGG HAD BEEN a patient of theirs all of his life. Cathy had looked up his files earlier when James came through and together, they had run down the list of reasons for him consulting them. It seemed that Thomas kept himself to himself and had not been in attendance for some years, but he had seen the practice nurse once for an infected toenail and she had referred him, quite rightly, to the podiatrist after that.

'Well,' James said, straightening up from the screen. 'Not much to be said. Poor chap. Moderate learning disability, that's all. I'd not have put him down as a person to kill, and there's nothing in his notes to suggest violent behaviour.'

'I might dig out his paper notes later,' Cathy said.

The practice still kept ancient physical notes in one of the back storerooms. These were mostly historical and of little interest to the GPs, but the police might quite well want to see them.

'Something from his paediatric files, you think?' James asked.

'Not really. I mean, how could there be anything? But you know what the police are like when they're making a case, and if it gets to the point where they charge him with murder, it'll all have to be gone through. He must have been assessed early on for learning disability, and surely well-known to the social work department. I guess that they'll find out more from them rather than us.'

'I wonder what evidence they have against him,' James mused.

'Didn't Julie say that the police were seen looking around the bins up at The Court? Perhaps they found something?'

Before James left, she asked him about the hospital. It had been playing on her mind a good deal and until now, she hadn't had a chance.

'Fernibanks?' James asked. 'Oh, it was shut a long time before you came, I suppose. Yes. There was an accident as it happens. A massive fire. Well, when I say massive, it involved only one building. A psychiatry consultant died. I don't know much about it though. I was locuming as a newly qualified GP back then and hadn't taken on the partnership yet. Eric might know, although it's years since we last spoke.' To Cathy's confused expression, he explained: 'I told you I went to one of those dreadful reunions years ago? Eric was a medical school friend. He ended up going into psychiatry for his sins, and I'm sure he was working there at some point.'

'If you get a chance, James, I'd be grateful if you could ask,' Cathy said.

James looked at her quizzically. 'Cathy? What's this all about then?'

She sighed and then smiled at his concern. 'I feel an obligation,' she admitted. 'Betty Scott was my patient and I let her down.'

James shook his head. 'No, Cathy.'

'She was worried about something, James, before she died. She mentioned her work as a nurse in the same conversation, and I just wondered ... She worked at Fernibanks; you see? Now is the first I've heard of this tragedy up there. What if the two deaths were linked in some way and the police are barking up the wrong tree?'

James snorted. 'They've got their man, Cathy. Poor Thomas Hogg. What do you want to go digging into it for?'

'I know,' she agreed. 'But James, do you honestly think that Thomas was responsible for Elizabeth Scott's death?'

James shrugged. 'It does seem unlikely.'

Cathy smiled triumphantly. 'Please speak to your friend?'

'Good excuse to hear Eric's news, I suppose,' he conceded.

James left her to it and for the rest of that morning, the two doctors consulted in rooms beside one another. Not unexpectedly, she received a call from the police mid-morning requesting a copy of Thomas's medical records. In a serious case such as this, confidentiality had to be waived and Cathy agreed.

'Of course. I'll look for his historical ones myself when I'm finished consulting. One of the girls will photocopy them for you if it helps.'

The police officer thanked her.

'Are you really convinced he did it?' she asked.

The man sighed. 'Difficult, but it seems highly likely. It's uncomfortable for all of us, but there it is. Sometimes I wonder how many of these people do slip through the net. He's been next to useless in interviews. Sits rocking and counting to himself most of the time. If he did kill her, he'll probably go where he should have been in the first place. An institute. Shouldn't have been roaming about on the streets.'

Cathy felt quite sick.

Following her morning surgery, she set to work through in the back room. It was rare to come into the store as most of the relevant patient notes were now computerised. When Cathy opened the door, the room smelt musty and the air was cold. She flicked on the light and sighed seeing the lines of dusty paper folders on the shelves.

'Oh Dr Moreland, you gave me a fright,' Michelle said as she passed the door.

'Sorry, Michelle,' Cathy said. 'I was just having a rummage.'

'If you do need a hand looking, give me or Julie a shout,' she offered, but Cathy was glad to be alone.

The room itself had no windows, and the only lighting was a fluorescent strip that seemed to flicker intermittently. Several times, Cathy looked skyward wondering if a moth was caught in the light shield, but it seemed that the electrical connection was poor. The shelves segmented the room into rows. The metal ledges ran the whole length and went from floor to ceiling. It felt oppressive, but Cathy was only too willing to make the sacrifice.

She came to 'H' and slowly began to look through. There were so many patients' surnames beginning with the letter. It was impossible to read the spines of the folders so Cathy was forced to withdraw each in turn until she neared the 'H-O's.' 'Hobbs,' 'Hodd,' 'Hodge.' She knew that she was getting close. Finally, she found 'Hogg,' and amazingly, it was where it was meant to be. There were two files. Thomas's was there as she had hoped, along with a woman called Flora Hogg. Cathy removed both and instead of examining them there, carried them back to her room where the lighting was better.

She started, of course, with Thomas. He appeared to have been seen a good deal in his former years. Paediatrics had assessed him on and off throughout his time at school, although it seemed from the notes, that he had not fully engaged with the education system. No specific label had been given to his disability. It was simply referred to as 'global delay'. At the age of six, his fine-motor and gross-motor skills had plateaued. His speech and language skills, along with his ability to learn, had stopped some time before. On several occasions, the notes mentioned a poor home life and lack of stability.

Cathy continued to read and found that in his teens, Thomas

had been referred urgently for psychiatric assessment following concern from a neighbour. The boy had been apparently, 'talking gibberish', and behaving aggressively to passersby. Thomas was documented as being restless on assessment and melancholy at times also, talking of 'ending his life with a blade.' It seemed that he had been put on a strong tranquilliser and sent home without follow-up.

Cathy leaned back in her chair and sighed. How things had changed. Poor Thomas. She felt for him, and all the other confused, young people who had gone through the system and been mismanaged.

There was little else to find. Thomas had been lost to the system for some time. In his late teens though, he was noted as behaving aggressively and in a sexually inappropriate manner towards a doctor. Cathy wondered if the police would read this and wonder if it was the start of something sinister. She thought it unlikely. It wasn't uncommon for young people with learning disability to become frustrated, especially if they were misunderstood. These days, the health service was so much better prepared to deal with such difficulties.

Before she moved onto the other file, James came to the door.

'You found them then?' he asked, seeing her sitting with the dusty files on her desk. 'Michelle said the police rang. I assume they want a copy?'

Cathy nodded. 'I'll get Michelle to do it in a minute. Painful reading, I'm afraid. Things were pretty insensitively documented back then. Words like 'imbecile', were banded about a good deal.'

James nodded. 'It would have been worse a generation before. His mother. You'd not have come across her though. I think she's alive actually, and still registered with us, but possibly now in a nursing home. Don't think I've been out to see her in a good while, though. She was locked up for most of her life. Much the same as poor Thomas mentally, but treated appallingly.'

'These will be her notes then,' Cathy said. 'Flora Hogg?'

'That's her. Don't get me wrong, she was always a very difficult person to deal with, but, well, that was the way things were done, I suppose, back then.'

Cathy smiled sadly. 'You going up for coffee, James? I'll head up in a minute, I just want to finish here.'

James left her to it. Cathy was unsurprised when she read that Flora Hogg had been a detainee in Fernibanks psychiatric hospital for almost all of her adult life. Then, at the age of fifty, she was released to a nursing home on the outskirts of Glainkirk.

Cathy gazed out of the window. Was this the connection between Betty Scott and Thomas? Had the young boy visited his mother in the hospital and known the matron? Had there been some bad feeling between the two? The link was tenuous, but resentments, when they ran deep, were often intensified over time. Cathy still wasn't convinced that Thomas Hogg was a killer, but she had proved the link and perhaps the police might do the rest.

## 18

The nursing home could not have been called salubrious. It was positioned down by the old mill that had long since been converted to flats. Cathy parked her car and sat for a moment wondering what she was doing there. James would be furious if he knew that she had ignored his plea. Over coffee, he had again suggested that she leave it alone. 'They aren't as daft as you make out,' he had laughed. 'If Thomas is innocent, then you need to trust that they'll find him so. That's how it works, Cathy.' She told him about the officer's comments on the phone. James grimaced. 'Not helpful,' he agreed. 'But we've enough on our plate without adding murder investigations to our workload.'

She knew he was right, of course, but when she came down from the coffee room to find that Linda had already taken the only two visits, leaving her free until after lunch, she set her jaw. Well, what harm would it do to have a conversation with someone?

Flora Hogg hadn't requested a visit in nearly two years. According to her notes, she had only a single recording of mild hypertension and had refused her flu vaccination every year that it had been offered. Just as well she had come out, Cathy justified. The poor lady had been neglected dreadfully by the practice.

'I'll warn you,' the woman said as they now stood together in the foyer. 'Flora isn't the easiest to talk to. Never been keen on men, and not a fan of doctors either.'

'I'll be as sensitive as I possibly can,' Cathy said. 'I see from her notes that she rarely asks to be seen.'

'That's right,' the woman said as she led Cathy through the building. The corridors were narrow, and along them, a handrail was positioned on either side.

'How long has she been a resident?' Cathy asked the back of the other woman's head.

'Nearly eleven years. I was just glancing over her notes before you arrived as it happens. Here we are,' she said as they came level with one of the many doors in the corridor. 'Usually, she likes to go to the television room in the morning but today she's in her bedroom.' The woman knocked. 'Can we come in Flora? Just me and a nice lady to visit, like I told you.'

Cathy wasn't quite sure what she had expected. Flora Hogg sat on the edge of her bed. She was a squat, rounded sort of a woman, and her face was a deep red. Her eyes seemed to be constantly moving and when Cathy introduced herself, the eyes flicked over towards her, and then away again, across the room, never resting on a single thing.

Cathy thanked the woman who had shown her through.

'I'll wait just outside the door if you don't mind,' she said. 'I'm sure Flora will be just fine, but there have been issues in the past.'

Cathy nodded. 'If I need anything ...' she said and the woman closed the door.

Cathy looked across at Flora, trying to judge how best to begin. 'Your room,' she said, 'it's pretty.' There were no photographs at all. She looked at the curtains and the matching bedspread. 'You like flowers?' she asked and Flora's eyes skimmed the top of Cathy's head but didn't settle. 'Do you have a favourite?' she asked, sitting on the chair by the bed.

Flora sniffed and seemed to be deciding on whether she should speak. 'Roses,' she finally said. Her voice was slightly lisped.

Cathy grinned. 'Well, you're a great romantic then,' she said. 'Roses are not only beautiful, but they smell good too. I'll bet you get a lovely view from your window of the garden. Do they have many flowers here?'

Flora shrugged.

'It's too cold for growing much just now,' Cathy continued. 'But Spring isn't far off. It's my favourite season. New life. Baby lambs in the fields.' Cathy looked across at Flora, trying to gauge how the other woman felt. But Flora was scowling.

'I don't like babies.'

'No,' Cathy went on. 'Sometimes they are tiresome.'

'Crying and causing bother. Making me want to scream myself,' Flora said, her face deepening in colour to a near-purple.

Cathy felt that she had chosen the wrong line in discussion and quickly changed course. 'We've not seen you in a while. Not in ages. I had wanted to check and see how you were doing. I know you don't take any tablets these days, but I thought we could give you a look-over and see if your blood pressure was good. I expect it will be. You clearly take care of yourself and the people here seem very nice.'

Flora turned and for the first time, looked at Cathy.

'Who are you?' she asked.

'I'm sorry, I thought I'd said. I'm Cathy. Dr Moreland.'

Flora suddenly clasped her hands to her ears and without warning, began moaning. Cathy watched in horror as the poor woman rocked and cried, her shouts becoming louder and more insistent.

The door to Flora's room opened and the other woman walked in. 'Not to worry,' she said crossing the room. 'I thought this might happen. Now, now, Flora. Not to worry.' She turned to Cathy. 'Does she really need this now? She's had enough of doctors to last her a lifetime.'

Cathy got up. 'I didn't realise,' she said. 'No, it can wait. It was simply a routine check. Perhaps I can leave a blood pressure monitor …' But the other woman was wrapping her arms around Flora and rocking with her. 'I'll leave you in peace. I'm very sorry.'

She glanced back as she left the room. What a pitiful sight Flora Hogg made. What on earth had caused her to react so dramatically at the mention of her being a doctor? Cathy thought that she knew. Life must have been unpleasant for many residents at Fernibanks, and poor Flora Hogg had been incarcerated for nearly her entire adult life. It made her feel quite sick.

As she crossed the car park, now glad to be outside, she wondered if she had learned anything at all from the visit. Flora Hogg had without question, been an unsuitable person to mother a child given what she had said. But where did that leave things with her son Thomas? Had Thomas been to visit his mother in Fernibanks all those years ago? Had he witnessed his only known relative's distress and possible ill-treatment at Betty's hands as she worked there as the matron? Had he harboured a grudge against the old woman? Cathy just wasn't convinced.

# 19

It was Neil who greeted Holly at the door. He stood, partially blocking her entrance. Had she wanted to try; she would have to pass too close to his horrible figure. Holly was unsure what he was playing at, until he looked up and down the street like some rubbish mime artist, and then bent in closer.

'Before you go in,' he said conspiratorially, 'I heard that you've been seen hanging around with a murderer. They're saying it's crazy Thomas. Don't suppose he confessed to you then, did he?'

'Piss off, Neil,' she said and pushed past. His body felt like a rack of empty coat-hangers, shifting and clattering. It took Holly an eternity to shake off the violation.

The shop was yet to open, but it seemed that most of the volunteers had arrived in good time to get things organised. Everyone assumed that they would be busy. It was a reasonable supposition given the material on offer to local gossips, and the shop was, of course, at the centre of it all. Perhaps they might take advantage of the situation and make a huge profit that day.

'Morning,' Alex called through from the kitchen, and Holly realised that it was the first time she had seen him since he plied her with alcohol the other night. She was slightly unsure of how to behave, but he made it easy, stepping out of the room and grinning. His hair was newly cut and Holly saw that he was greying slightly at the temples. It suited him, in a way.

'You left some shopping at mine,' he said, still smiling. Fortunately, Neil was out of earshot. If he had been there, he would have winked and jogged her in the ribs like a complete weasel. Holly walked through and hung her jacket on a peg at the back.

'Keep it,' she said to him, indicating the proffered bag. She wrestled with a hanger of tabards that had been freshly washed and ironed. When she turned back, he looked uncertain. It was as if she had slighted him, so as she walked back through, she told him she was going sober for the rest of the month and he laughed at that.

The morning was busy, as they had anticipated. It seemed that the charity shop was the hub of the community that day. Carbolic came in just after nine, keen to gloat over the arrest of his arch-enemy. He brought with him, a packet of Wagon Wheels and said that it was a gift after what they had all been through. Holly had no idea how a marshmallowy biscuit would help them get over the horrific death of a colleague, but she supposed it was the thought that counted.

Carol was her usual ingratiating self with Carbolic, maybe it was just to spite Holly. Perhaps only she saw the man's true motive for bringing in the treats. He was, of course, muscling in on Thomas's patch, and toading up to Carol so that he could establish himself as a favourite. Holly couldn't understand how they were all blind to it.

Holly was sure that Carbolic knew she couldn't tolerate him, as much out of loyalty to her new friend, as anything else. He tried to catch her eye while he was waving the shiny, red packet of biscuits around but she wouldn't be drawn. She heard his voice prattling on and on from the back room later, with him detailing how the police had arrived late-afternoon to go through the bins at the back of The Court. Presumably, they were looking for bloodstained clothing, for if Betty had been walloped on the head before being thrown on the railway, the perpetrator must have been in a bit of a state.

Even Alex noticed that Holly was off form and asked if she was alright, but she couldn't be bothered explaining herself. Part of her wasn't sure about trusting in anyone too hurriedly. As she upended bag after bag onto the floor, she found herself reflecting. To be fair, there wasn't much to go on, but she was inflexible in her belief that Thomas was innocent.

Holly thought of what she had learned about the lives of the other volunteers, and how Betty's interactions with them had been less doddery and passive, and more ominous than she had originally supposed. Betty had been a dubious character, and it appeared to be quite possible that she had stirred up trouble, certainly for Neil. Then there was the blazing row with Carol also. Betty had at one time, been a matron. It must have been a position of great responsibility. How might she have taken Carol's constant needling and micromanaging?

Of course, there was always a possible link to the fire up at the old psychiatric building and the death of the psychiatrist all those years ago. It seemed significant that all of this had kicked off after Neil's horrible tale too. Holly cast her mind back to when Neil had shown around his newspaper cutting. She recalled everyone's polite interest, but Betty had looked like she had seen a ghost. What did it all mean?

Straightening up from her bundle of assorted clothes, Holly sighed. She couldn't stand the back room any longer. She crossed the corridor and came to stand in the kitchen doorway. The room was even more chaotic than usual. Alex, despite his preference to sort books, had stepped in to help Neil, as things it seemed, had begun to get rather out of hand.

Alex looked at her and smiled.

'I can't settle,' she said and shrugged.

'Thomas?' he asked.

She nodded and hoped he wouldn't be too nice to her.

'They'll keep a close eye on him,' he said, and glanced behind her, presumably in case someone was listening. Holly came further into the room and they stood huddled together. 'I know you felt sorry for the guy,' Alex said quietly, 'but if they do release him, it's probably best not to be seen hanging around chatting and being too friendly. That's my advice, but you can ignore it of course.'

Holly nodded. 'But even if the blood outside his flat was Betty's, it hardly points the finger directly at him, does it?'

Alex sighed. 'True, but they'll be looking for more evidence. If they're still waiting on forensic tests, they'll probably keep Thomas under some kind of surveillance, and even have him come into the station daily, just to make sure he doesn't do a runner.'

Holly snorted at this. 'Where would he go?'

'I suppose he is a vulnerable person too, so he might conceivably be a suicide risk,' Alex said.

Holly's stomach lurched.

'Cosy in here, you two?' Neil said, suddenly appearing and squeezing his way into the kitchen. 'Thought the pair of you'd been getting a bit chummy. Hope I've not missed anything exciting. They do say that tragedy brings people together. Now you have a common enemy in Thomas, who knows what could blossom?'

Holly hated the vile man, and out of spite more than anything, she ignored him completely.

'This evening, Alex?' she said, with a wicked glint in her eye. 'Your place. Eight o'clock? I won't bring a bottle because I know you've got.'

'I thought it was dry January?' Alex asked.

'Like hell it is. You'd better not have any plans for tomorrow because we're getting off our faces, and we'll be of no use to anyone.'

Neil looked like a school kid who had just lost his best mate, but Holly was already counting the hours until she could forget her concerns and slip happily into oblivion. It helped of course, that her co-conspirator wasn't a complete idiot, but she supposed, had Alex turned her down, she might quite easily have spent the night alone.

Admittedly, drowning her sorrows had become a bit of a habit, but the past few weeks had tested her to the limit. She had already decided that once this God-forsaken business was cleared up, she'd be packing her bags and leaving. She might never find out what she came for originally, but she owed it to Betty to stick it out. Alcohol would help. It always did.

After leaving the shop, having re-established with Alex that he'd better get the glasses ready, Holly turned back down the high street in the opposite direction.

The evening was cold and she drew her jacket tight around. He fell in step beside her, without her notice. She had no idea how long they walked together; her mind furiously engaged in the unfairness of it all. When she glanced sideways, it had been because of his shadow as they passed together under a street light. He was perhaps a couple of steps behind. Holly had no idea if he intended to announce himself, or if he would have followed her the entire way up to the old psychiatric hospital in silence.

Instead of turning to look, she continued to walk but with more purpose. The thud of the wheels as they skated over the paving slabs was impossible to ignore. When she could stand it no more, she stopped dead in the street and spun around. He leapt back and teetered on the edge of the pavement, his arms flailing.

'Why are you following me?' she asked.

'I'm not,' he replied, but his immediate smirk gave him away. 'I've not seen you in ages,' he said. 'I wanted a news.'

'I'm heading home,' she told him.

'You're not. This is the wrong way. Why are we going up to the old hospital anyway? I always hated it here.'

Holly ignored this and he shrugged. They set off once more.

'I heard about the police,' Holly said, half-turning as he still insisted on following up the hill. 'I thought you were still being questioned.'

He tutted, and then perhaps realising that he was duty-bound to give her something more, stated: 'Oh aye. You did hear then.'

He laughed a bit after that. The kind of insane laugh that made her wonder if he knew the seriousness of what had occurred. Once he had finished with the laughing, he told her that he was thinking about something else. Holly didn't ask what.

'Stop walking behind,' she said, already finding herself irritated by the man and his carry-on. 'People were worried about you, you know?'

'You mean, you were worrying?' Thomas asked, still lagging annoyingly back.

'I wasn't worried at all,' she said. 'I couldn't have cared less about you. The police might well have been torturing you and I wouldn't have thought a thing about it. It was Marie, I meant. Don't you care?' she asked, stopping and spinning around on him once more. 'You could have been arrested for murder. You still might be. Doesn't that frighten you? Blood was found outside your home. You're only free now because they don't have enough evidence yet.'

Holly studied his pock-marked face in the yellowish light. He met her gaze for a moment and then looked at his feet. 'I know, I know,' he said.

Tears stung at her eyes and she wiped them angrily with the sleeve of her jacket. She felt like she had just beaten a wretched dog with a stick. She turned again and began walking. This time, he didn't follow. She got beyond the next street light when he called out, and despite herself, she smiled.

'I thought you were finding who did it anyway,' he shouted. 'I wasn't worried 'cos I knew you were on my side.'

## 20

It was well past eight when Holly arrived at Alex's. She wondered if he'd be a bit annoyed, but when he opened the door, he was all politeness, and clearly ready to play the perfect host. After her unsatisfying conversation with Thomas, she was eager to start on a bottle of vodka but it seemed that she would have to at least pretend to be a normal human being first. This saddened her to some extent. She had thought that she and Alex were on the same wave-length. But when she went into the living room and saw that he had put coasters on the coffee table, she knew that he was far too nice a man for her.

'Have you started without me?' she asked, eyeing up a glass of something on the mantlepiece.

'Diet Coke,' he said. 'I was waiting. I take it you're on the hard stuff? I have a good whisky in the cupboard. Don't really drink it myself, it was a gift.'

'Can't stand the stuff,' she told him. 'I've brought my own anyway.' She held up the vodka. 'But I'll mix it. No offence,' she said. Perhaps he thought she was accusing him of wanting to date-rape her or something. 'I'm fussy like that,' she explained, 'and you'll be polite and give me too much mixer.'

Holly followed him through to the kitchen. Part of her died a little when she saw that the table was set for two and he had already put the oven on.

'Just pizza,' he said, probably seeing the panic in her eyes.

'I've had half a loaf of bread before coming,' she told him, and he laughed.

'You're a bit of a pro then?'

Things, of course, became more relaxed when Holly's Russian comrade began to take effect. She was on her third glass when her muscles started to soften and her jaw became lax. Alex, she noted, was taking things more leisurely, and even with her undisguised enthusiasm for the drink, he appeared less forthcoming.

'What a week,' Holly said, as they sat now in the living room at her suggestion, with plates of pizza on their knees, instead of at his more formal arrangement next-door.

'What? Betty and the shop and all?' he asked, wiping his mouth with a piece of kitchen roll.

'Yeah. It's a bloody mess. I was hoping you'd been helping the police out on the quiet,' she said. 'Maybe undercover at the charity shop. I know you said you were a retired officer or whatever, but that might have been a ruse to put me off.'

Alex snorted and shook his head. 'No, but I've been thinking about what you said earlier in the shop, about the blood. Do you remember, when we were in the kitchen talking about Thomas being questioned?'

Holly looked up. 'What did I say? I can't remember what I was thinking about two seconds ago.'

'Just about them finding blood in The Court and it not necessarily meaning it was him. That it could easily be any one of the residents there. It reminded me of a thing I heard. Purely gossip, though, so nothing of any importance.'

By now. Holly had placed her plate on the floor and looked at Alex with real interest.

'No, don't get excited,' he said. 'It's just about that man who comes in the shop. Carbolic, they call him. You know who I mean?'

She nodded.

'Well, I heard about him a while back. Think he used to work on the bins or something and got fired for coarse behaviour. Anyway, it's just I heard he had a history of violence. Not sure if it led to a criminal record or not, but there was talk of it, I'm sure. It was just a thing I had in the back of my head,' Alex said smiling. 'The police will be onto it though, of course.'

Holly took a swig of the vodka. 'It's funny you mentioning him, because only the other day, Carol was talking about him too.'

Alex leaned forward and moved one of the unused table mats so that it was in line with the right-angle of the table. Holly glanced down in disbelief.

'She said that she'd come across him in the past. Years and years ago, she said, in her line of work.'

'Oh?' Alex asked. 'I can't imagine Carol in a real job. What did she do then?'

'She used to be a social worker, apparently.'

Alex looked incredulous.

'I know, I know, she must have been a nightmare,' Holly laughed. 'Goodness knows how they managed to boot her out. Probably interfering in too many folks' business, I imagine.'

Alex snorted. 'I never knew, but then why would I? So, she looked after that man Carbolic, did she? And what did she have to say about him?'

'Funnily enough, pretty much the same as you. History of

violent temper. He was a hoarder by the sounds of things. Had to be forcibly removed from his house. Rats everywhere.'

'So Carbolic's our best bet, is he?' Alex asked.

'You're the ex-policeman,' she laughed. 'What do you think about the rest of the charity shop workers? Anyone got a good motive? Didn't you say you saw Betty rowing with both Neil and Carol on separate occasions?'

At this, Alex looked like he had a secret to tell. He smirked a bit and went all shy.

'Oh, come on, don't pretend you're not going to tell me,' she said 'I thought we were pals. You're about the only person I can abide in that bloody place.'

'Why do you stay on then?' he asked.

'God knows,' she said, 'but don't try and distract me. You know something, don't you?'

Alex picked up his now empty plate and getting up, he retrieved hers.

'I don't do crusts,' she said in explanation. 'Stop messing about,' she called after him, as he went through to the kitchen. He returned grinning.

'You're a bit impatient, aren't you?' he asked. 'OK, so I do know something, but this is strictly between the two of us. I've no grudge to bear against Neil, and if anything, I quite like the man and our silly chats. Oh, I know he's got an ego the size of Britain, but I think he's as insecure as the next man, if not more so.'

'OK,' she told him. 'Pinkie promise I won't tell a soul.'

'So, I did overhear Betty and Neil talking. It would have been weeks and weeks before she died though, and it was only a little snippet too, but it finally made sense the other day in the shop. I asked him about it. It seems that Betty caught him. He wasn't doing anything illegal,' Alex said quickly. 'But to be fair it was immoral, and even I struggle a bit with it, but that's probably the 'done' thing in the antique business.'

Holly was beginning to get quite irritated by this preamble.

He grinned. 'OK, I'll get to it,' he said. 'So, it seems that Neil has never hidden the fact that he used to run a successful antique business. When he retired, he could have put his feet up quite comfortably, but my guess is, that when you've done that kind of a job, it's hard to switch off. You must see potential deals everywhere.'

Holly took another slug of the vodka but didn't take her eyes off Alex's face.

'Yes, so he must have offered his services in the charity shop on the pretext of keeping himself busy. I don't think that part of it's a lie anyway. But, and even Neil admitted this to me the other day when I pressed him, things have come in through that shop. These have been legitimate donations that you or I might well discount as being worthless. We could have stuck a one-pound tag on them, without knowing any better, but Neil has spotted something more.'

'Has he stolen something?' Holly asked.

'Oh, God no, not at all. I told you, it wasn't illegal. But in the past, when things have come in, he's seen their real value. He told me it was mostly jewellery. It would be stuff that looked like coloured glass to you or me, but Neil would have known through his experience in the antique trade, that whatever it was, was worth a lot more.'

'And so, he mislabeled them?' she asked.

'I don't think it even got as far as that. He might not have even put them out on the shop floor at all, but gone to the person on the till, saying he wanted to buy them for his wife, or whatever. He'd have purchased them for next-to-nothing, planning to resell them online probably, and would have gone on to make a sweet little profit.'

Holly shook her head in disbelief. 'Crafty bugger,' she said.

'Immoral as I said, but not illegal.'

'And I suppose Betty realised and threatened to get him kicked out of the shop?'

'Pretty much,' Alex said. 'As I say, he's told me about it and it's not as if Betty could have blackmailed him or anything, but it's a rather nice, little earner on the side for him, and it would have been a shame to ruin it, as he put it, all because the old woman was feeling moralistic.'

'Well,' Holly said, leaning back and sighing. 'Neil does seem to be in the frame. And I so wished it could be Carol. I've never met such an annoying woman in my life.'

Alex laughed and they topped up their drinks once more.

'I suppose it could have been her,' he said, 'just playing devil's advocate.'

'Go on then, why Carol?' Holly asked. It was good to have someone to talk to about it all. She had bounced the ideas around her head enough times to give herself a concussion.

'Well then,' said Alex, leaning back on the sofa. 'She and Betty didn't get on, did they? Betty had been in that shop and running things for far longer than her. How do you think it must have felt when Carol waltzed in and started re-organising things? You know how bossy Carol can be? Imagine how galling that would have been for Betty.'

'It's not enough to kill for though,' she said disappointedly. 'And anyway, that would be a motive for Betty killing Carol.'

Alex scrunched up his face and looked as if he was thinking hard. 'OK, how about Betty overheard Carol and Tricia, or whoever, discussing the shop takings. Maybe the shop's been doing much worse than Carol makes out.'

'We're always busy though,' she said.

'Good point.' Alex put his glass down. 'Right, so how about this?' he said. 'Maybe takings shouldn't be down, but maybe

Carol has been managing the shop very badly indeed, not paying overheads, heating bills, or whatever. Remember she hired that skip? They cost a bloody fortune; you know? How the charity agreed to it, I've no idea. So maybe she's been overspending, and Betty threatened to go to head-office about it. How about that?'

'I like that one better,' Holly said. 'You're far cleverer at this than me.'

Finally, she felt at peace. After all of Alex's nonsense earlier with the bloody tablemats and the pizza, Holly had begun to worry that she might have misjudged him. For the rest of that night, he wasn't nearly so uptight and even when he tried to kiss her as she left, he took the slap in good spirit, and even told her that he deserved it.

## 21

When Holly woke it was nearly midday. She was surprised to be completely free of a headache and only the slightest taste of vomit played on her lips. Getting up, she explored her surroundings. She was glad to find that she had had the foresight after months of rehearsal, to place a pint of water by her bedside. The kitchen and bathroom were more chaotic. A trail of her clothes led from the front door, now a well-established routine. Her jacket lay, its arm outstretched in a beckoning, come-hither manner. Her top, jeans and underwear were less comically displayed, and when she did finally bother to pick up and redistribute the mess, she found that a sock was missing. God knows what had become of it.

But the truth of the matter was, that she was far less indisposed than she should have been that morning, and for very good reason. Holly wasn't a complete idiot after all. She trusted Alex no more than the rest of the charity shop bunch and going to his house on the pretext of letting her hair down had been, of course, part of the plan. She had perhaps let herself relax a little too much and that was unfortunate, but had she gone all out on the vodka as he had thought she was doing, she would have been incapable of self-defence, and might easily have ended up unconscious on his living room floor.

Considering that Alex was still very much a suspect, Holly had decided to water-down some of her drinks the previous night and had determined never to allow Alex to mix one in case he slipped something into the glass. She had been facetious about him date-raping her, but one could never be too careful. To make doubly sure, on returning home, she had stuck her fingers down her throat. Good for cleansing the body of unwanted toxins.

As she padded around her small flat, unable to put the heating fully up due to her lack of credit, she thought over what she had gained through her alliance with Alex. He had been all too eager to come up with motives for his charitable colleagues. Admittedly, he had been egged on, and might well have been showing off, or trying to get into her good-books, but it did speak volumes about his character. Holly had never befriended a police officer before, but she wasn't so sure that this was normal behaviour for one, even if they had taken medical retirement. She thought back to what Alex had told her about his work and about how saddened he was to leave what he clearly saw as his vocation. Last night, he had become less inhibited, although she was quite aware that he was pacing himself and unwilling to completely let himself go. Towards the end of the evening, they had discussed his work once again. 'Eight years in February,' he had kept repeating. 'Eight bloody years.' It was at that point; when he appeared to be becoming maudlin, that she had decided to call it a night. Holly hated a miserable drunk having been one herself so many times before, and she didn't want her impression of Alex to be ruined.

In many ways, part of her didn't want to know the truth now. She sat at the kitchen table sipping at a freshly made mug of coffee, grimacing at the heat of it and staring at the blank computer screen. She wondered if what she was about to do was wise. Just then, a message flashed up on her mobile. It was from him. Some witty little check-in, clearly making sure that she was still talking to him. Holly wished he hadn't, because he came over all the more out of practice at these things. Having a romantic association had never been part of the plan, but perhaps she had led him on in some way. She still couldn't fathom what the man saw in her. Perhaps it was simple desperation. She was certainly in no place mentally to be carrying-on with anyone. It seemed all the odder though, given that she had told him next-to-nothing about herself still. The previous night, when he asked again about what she had done before coming to Glainkirk, she had made some trite comment and skirted the issue once more. Perhaps he was one of those men that liked a broken woman; someone to fix and then spend a lifetime accepting the adulation and gratitude they deserved. But that wasn't her thing at all.

Holly ignored the text message, and with this in mind, began her search. It was irritatingly easy to find and surprisingly so given the nature of the information. Within thirty minutes of trawling, clicking in and out of various regulatory documents, she had discovered what she was after. She found herself quite shocked by the list. Never before had she considered the possible reasons for a trusted official losing their job. It seemed that many people had gone rogue over the years. Her eyes immediately fell on one, which cited 'sexual relationship with a vulnerable female'. This she thought was bad enough, until she found: 'possession and taking indecent images of children'. Her blood ran cold. The others were similar but less sensational: 'drink driving', 'data protection offences', 'theft and selling counterfeit goods'. There was even a 'possession of cannabis' in there. Holly snorted as she read this.

She kept on scrolling, until she came to the correct date and area, as they had all been subdivided into regions of the country. It wasn't much, just a single line, and the name wasn't even mentioned, but she knew it had to be him. On the disapproved register, for gross misconduct, was a police constable. The reason given for his dismissal from the college of policing was: 'unreasonable use of force."

In a way, it was a relief that he wasn't a paedophile, or anything really bad, but it was still shocking to see it in print. Holly considered again their conversation from the previous night, and how he had done his big dramatic disclosure of why Carbolic should be considered a possible suspect for Betty's murder. He had said that the man had a history of violence, and this might predispose him to further crime. It now seemed that Alex also fell into this category. She wondered at his hypocrisy in saying what he had, but then he had assumed that history might stay as such and that his past would be unlikely to come out.

Holly sipped meditatively on her now stone-cold coffee. The bitterness seemed to be more exaggerated, but it fitted her mood just fine. She wondered how on earth she was going to face Alex again, knowing now what she did. It wasn't so much the actual reason for him being booted out of the force that bothered her, it was more the fact that he had deliberately lied. She did wonder though, what 'unreasonable use of force' meant. Had he punched a suspect too hard, perhaps initially in self-defence, or had it been much worse? You saw in the paper these reports of corrupt cops lording it up. Pumped up on power and reckless because of it. She hated to think of Alex in that way, but perhaps when he was younger, it might have been the case. If it had been so, then what a comedown, ending up in this town, and working for free, with a collection of no-hopers like herself. She marvelled at his strength of character, really, she did.

It was gone three o'clock when she finally washed and

dressed. The bathroom required a bit of attention from the previous evening's purging incident, but she was in no mood to attend to it and instead avoided the sink completely and brushed her teeth as she washed her hair in the shower. From the frosted bathroom window, she gazed out at the greying-yellow sky. The clouds had a bilious tinge to them, which probably meant snow.

Given that the heating had now gone off completely and with little money to spare, she decided that bed wasn't such a bad place to be. She scooped up a book from the floor and was reading, having found comfort in the cocoon of quilt when she heard a bell ringing. Initially, she ignored it, thinking that it must be the neighbours again. They regularly forgot their keys or had guests visiting, coming loudly up the stairs at some ridiculous time of night. Granted, it was only five in the afternoon, but she wasn't getting up for anyone. The bell continued to sound. The perpetrator, becoming presumably irritated, had begun to press out a rhythm, allowing, at intervals, the bell to resonate in one long, steady and constant blast.

Holly swore, and throwing off the covers, stalked to the door.

'What?' she shouted in the intercom as the bell continued. The din stopped and she heard a crackling and shuffling, and then someone cleared their throat.

'Well then? Who is it?' she shouted again.

'Aye, aye,' came the hesitant reply.

Swearing loudly, she pressed the buzzer to allow him entry to the building. What a bloody joke it all was. How the man had found the flat was beyond her. He had probably followed at a distance the other evening, just to see where she lived, the devious swine. Holly was in no humour for visitors and even his pitiful reticence as he came into view, ambling up the stairs, with his ugly bag still in tow, did nothing to lift her spirits.

'Well then,' she said perversely, 'why have you come?'

He stood on the doorstep, shuffling his feet and doing that strange thing he did; tilting his head to the side and then taking a great sniff of air.

One of the people from an upstairs flat passed by, forcing him to step closer to her doorway. She nodded at the neighbour, who returned a raised eyebrow. Thomas's proximity was nauseating, and she turned her head in disgust and stepped back to allow for more room between them. Thinking that this was an invitation, he made as if to come in, but she was adamant that that wasn't happening.

'No way,' she said firmly, ushering him back. 'What do you want anyway?'

He began to chuckle to himself, something she had admittedly witnessed before, but it did not ease the nastiness of the situation. His body shuddered in great, awkward heaves, which was even more disconcerting as he was still so close. His snorting and crowing seemed to go on forever, and she fell into the trap of asking what was so funny. But he had no idea, and if anything, seemed slightly surprised, and then defensive when put on the spot.

For the first time, she noticed that his jacket was ripped at the sleeve and the stuffing, once presumably white, spilt frothy and discoloured. It reminded her of the water Carol washed down the sink after cleaning the shop floor.

'Have you been in a fight?' she asked. 'Well, what do you have to say?'

He shook his head as if trying to remove the question. He shifted from foot to foot again, and then held his hands up to his ears, covering them. His hands were mottled from the cold, like uncooked meat.

'Numbers, numbers. They're everywhere but how do I know which one's mine? Maybe I've missed it. I saw an eight, but maybe it wasn't for me. What time is it now?'

Holly's jaw tightened.

'Think I'll probably wake up dead tomorrow,' he remarked suddenly, with self-satisfied resolve.

'Don't be ridiculous,' she retorted. 'Has this got something to do with the police? Have they questioned you again?'

He looked at her keenly, as if trying to read her thoughts. The entire encounter, she knew was hopeless though. The man was intoxicated and unable to have any kind of conversation at all.

'Go home,' she told him. 'Go and sober up.'

His eyes swivelled, adjusting and readjusting, flitting from one thing to the next. Holly wondered if he was seeing something that she could not.

'I know who did it,' he finally said, turning the words into song, and again went off onto one of his roaring guffaws.

'You don't know, do you Thomas?' she asked.

He shook his head in bemusement as if only seeing her for the first time.

'I can't deal with this just now,' she told him and closed the door in his face.

## 22

'So, you're onto another murder are you, darling? I thought you'd be sick of them by now, having already had a few too many brushes with death this last year. When I saw the report on TV, I must say that I did think of you. Well then, have you solved the thing, or are you still burrowing into the mishmash of lies and intrigue?'

Cathy laughed and placed her glass of wine on the table. Suzalinna had invited her over as Saj was on-call that evening. 'A chance to dissect the reunion,' she had said, given that the two friends hadn't managed to see one another since.

'Well,' Cathy said, leaning in. 'The police have arrested someone.'

'Have they? And who is it? Not a patient of yours, along with the victim?'

'Oh God, well, when you say it like that, it does sound dreadful,' Cathy said. 'Yes, as it happens, they were both patients of ours, but the man arrested, or rather, I think he's being questioned, hasn't seen either James or me in years. A local man with a mild-to-moderate learning disability.'

'Really? And is he the right man?' Suzalinna asked, now topping up both of their glasses of wine.

Cathy grimaced.

'Oh, so you're not convinced?'

Cathy sighed and replaced her glass on the table. 'The old lady who died came in to see me. It was before the reunion thing and I was so worried about it that night, that I nearly mentioned it to you. She had breast cancer and didn't have long to live. She was refusing treatment, as it happens, but something was concerning her. She told me that it was something to do with the charity shop in town. Someone was disturbed or dangerous, she said. It had rattled her, but she wouldn't say any more than that. Said that I was her insurance policy if something went wrong, and it certainly has now.'

'Charity shop?' Suzalinna asked. 'I don't understand.'

'That's where she volunteered.'

'Had she always worked there?'

'No, she used to be the matron at Fernibanks.'

'The old psychiatric place?'

'Yes. I wondered if she had seen someone in the charity shop, or if something had happened recently to concern her. Something that brought back a memory from her old days working in the hospital. I got the impression that she had been watching someone for a while. Maybe weighing up if she should do something. It was as if she knew someone was a danger, but … Oh, I don't even know, it's all supposition, and none of it makes any sense.'

'Had this man who's been arrested, been into the shop? Was he a volunteer?'

'I doubt he would have been any use to them helping out. I don't think he's ever worked. I had a flick through his old paediatric notes. The police came in to collect them.'

'Grim reading?'

'Yes. Pretty sad. Treated like an animal, a drain on society, and his mother, who was also learning-disabled, was much the same, if not worse.'

'So, she's still alive, is she?'

'In a nursing home now. She's spent almost all of her life in an institution. She was in Fernibanks. I visited her in the hope of learning something more about her son, and his connection with the woman who died, but she couldn't tell me anything. To be frank, she was scared stiff when she realised I was medical.'

'That might be the connection then, don't you think? Perhaps this old lady, back in the day, was a bit of an evil one. You know it used to happen. Maybe she was cruel to the patients, including this poor lad's mother and he got to hear about it. Perhaps he's been waiting for his big chance to smack her over the head and throw her in front of a train.'

Cathy frowned. 'It's a bit excessive isn't it, and after all these years? Why now?'

'Well, if he got wind that she was dying, maybe he wanted to get in there first and bump her off in a horrible manner to spite her for what she had done.'

Cathy shook her head. 'Honestly, I don't think he'd have the mental capacity to come up with all of that. Why endanger himself when she was going to die anyway? It doesn't make sense.'

'Maybe she had a word. He'd been acting more and more strangely, and she told him she was going to get him locked up like his mother.'

'That sounds a bit more plausible. She was a bit of a tartar, but I still can't see him managing to lure the old woman down to the railway line. She would hardly go and meet him, knowing already that he was a danger, would she?'

'True enough,' Suzalinna conceded. 'Well, darling, it's a bit of a mess, I must say, but not your problem either. If the police have him already, and presumably they have reason ...?'

'Blood outside the sheltered housing complex where he lives. I think it's being tested still.'

'Well, darling. The case doesn't look great, does it?'

Cathy shook her head sadly. 'No, it doesn't look good.'.

'Anyway,' Suzalinna said, leaning forward and grinning. 'Onto other matters. I heard you pumping Sally Cruickshank at the reunion for info on her ex, the dishy policeman. I always knew you had a thing for that guy, even when they were going out all those years ago. Which, by the way, I knew wouldn't last. They were unsuited. He was far too timid for her, and I think slightly intimidated at our medics' do's. You and him though, well, that would have been another thing. What's happened to the handsome police officer then? Is he still in these parts, by any chance?'

Cathy snorted and refused to be drawn.

It was gone eleven when her cab arrived to take her home.

'Behave yourself and keep out of trouble,' Suzalinna warned, 'unless of course, it's with a man and then you have my permission to be as ill-disciplined as you like.'

Cathy kissed her friend and got into the taxi, promising to speak to her very soon.

The journey home would only take ten minutes. The taxi driver had turned on the radio, and the music was quiet and easy. Along with the motion of the car, it made Cathy sleepy. She looked out of the window as they went and recognised Davenport Road. The driver should indicate soon as they approached the corner where the old playground still stood. Half the swings had been spiralled over the beam so that they hung too short. They turned onto the road at right-angles now, and the slope of the street led them up. The headlights of the car caught a couple of people walking along the pavement. A little further on, the driver had to swerve as another car accelerated down the hill towards them. The taxi driver cursed under his breath but pulled his car expertly in behind a parked vehicle and out of the way before continuing. They were almost in line now with Fernibanks, and Cathy gazed out at the looming derelict hospital ahead, the buildings even darker against the night sky. Her eyes had become accustomed to the shadows now, and the sky had cleared a little as a cloud that had obliterated the moon shifted. The old hospital was lit up momentarily, a dilapidated monument to all of the troubled souls who had stayed there.

Then suddenly, and without warning, the driver swore loudly and jammed on the brakes. Cathy was thrown forward, and she felt her seatbelt seizing and restraining her torso. Instinctively, she put out her hands to protect her face. The car skidded, and the wheels on tarmac screamed. Cathy waited for a thump of metal on metal, expecting a collision, but there was none. When they stopped, there was an unnerving stillness.

'Are you alright, love?' asked the driver, turning breathlessly.

'Yes. What on earth?'

But the man was already getting out of the car, and Cathy after a moment, undid her belt and got out too. Her chest ached and she stumbled initially.

On the road in front of them, lay what looked like a sack. It was only as Cathy drew closer and the taxi driver stepped aside that she saw it was a man. He lay on his righthand side, his knees drawn up almost in a foetal position. His jacket was ripped and damp, and one of his shoes lay in the middle of the road as if carelessly discarded.

'Don't touch him!' Cathy shouted, and her voice sounded shrill.

The taxi driver straightened up. 'My God, it's Thomas Hogg,' he said. 'But I didn't hit him, he was lying there. I thought he was in with the police?'

'Call an ambulance,' she said.

She looked up and down the street in case they were in immediate danger from oncoming traffic, but the night was still. The only sound was of the occasional hiss of tyres on the high street as cars passed in the town below.

Cathy was already bending and gently uncovering the man's face. He was bleeding from a wound to his head, but it looked superficial. She quickly scanned his body and saw the twist to his left leg, but there were more important things to attend to before fractured limbs.

'Hello? Thomas? Can you hear me?' she asked. Cathy was at first concerned that he might be dead. In the background, she heard the driver on the phone, giving their location and explaining that they had found a man lying in the middle of the road, presumably the victim of a hit-and-run. 'He looks pretty bad,' Cathy heard him telling the operator, and his voice shook.

'Can you hear me, Thomas?' she asked again and thankfully the man groaned. 'Thank Goodness.'

The taxi driver was back. 'What should we do? Move him into the recovery position?'

'No. I need to stabilise his neck. I'm worried about his breathing though. I'm a doctor,' she said, glancing up at the driver.

'Thank Christ for that. I'll get a blanket from the cab. What else can I do?'

'Can you park the car so that we're protected from any oncoming traffic?' Cathy called, 'and keep the headlights on us.'

The driver moved away. Cathy had already noticed that Thomas's breathing was heavily laboured. It came in shallow heaves. As the headlights of the car moved, she saw too, now that the neck of his jacket was loose, that at his bare throat, his trachea was pulled to the side.

'Shit! How long until they said they'd be here?' she asked,

knowing that the man on the ground would die if they didn't hurry.

'Ten, fifteen minutes. They said to hang tight and they'd be here as fast as they could. I heard on the radio earlier that there was an accident on the Forkieth Road so they might be stuck.'

Cathy swore again. 'He's not going to survive if I don't do something. His lung's punctured. I don't have anything to help him.'

The man's breathing was now far more erratic and Cathy was very uneasy. Although it was dark, she could see the grey-blue cyanosis of his face.

'Have you got a pen?' she impulsively asked.

The driver looked incredulous.

'A biro is best,' she called after his retreating figure.

She had read in the past about a biro being used to treat a tension pneumothorax. It had been in a similar, life-or-death situation. It was the last thing she wanted to do to the poor man as he lay on the road, but if she didn't, he might well die before the ambulance arrived.

The driver came back. She had already covered Thomas's lower half with a blanket the driver had brought from the cab. Cathy, now shaking herself, with both cold and fear, took the pen.

'I need to unbutton his top, but I can't disturb his neck too much in case it's fractured,' she said.

The driver helped her. 'Thank goodness you were with me,' he said. 'I wouldn't have had a clue.'

'What I'm going to do will look brutal,' she warned him. 'You might want to look away.'

She had already located the midclavicular line with her fingers and counted down to the second rib, feeling for the second intercostal space. The man's chest creaked and rattled and she saw that now there was bruising forming along the lines of his chest and the air that was trying to enter, only sucked the skin tighter around the bones. Even touching lightly, revealed the uneven edge of the ribs where they had fractured.

'Thank God he's out of it,' the driver said.

The man on the ground continued to groan but indeed thankfully, seemed unaware of the situation.

'Look away now,' Cathy said as she positioned the pen.

It took a good deal more force than she had expected. The man shifted beneath her and grunted in pain. Then came the pop and release that she wanted. She nearly cried with relief. She withdrew the pen and took the middle part out, leaving just the plastic tube, which she placed in the hole she had punctured in his chest. She smiled, hearing the hiss of air escaping and watched as the man's breathing gradually started to come back to something almost like normal. At least he was out of immediate danger.

'Jesus,' the taxi driver said, and Cathy looked up.

'Never had to do that before,' she confessed. 'Hope I never have to again. Now, let's get this neck a bit more stable, and I'll be happier.'

The ambulance crew, when they finally arrived, were astounded to find Cathy's improvised chest drain in situ and the patient drifting in and out of consciousness.

'I've not done a top to toe,' Cathy said, 'but I was concerned about spine and pelvis. His left ankle's undoubtedly fractured. Obviously, he had a tension pneumothorax, so he'll need a more permanent drain when he gets to the hospital. Head scan too, I guess. He's been out of it. Strong smell of alcohol.'

It was only when the ambulance left, that Cathy began to shake uncontrollably.

'Better get you home,' the driver said. 'You're frozen through. It's a free ride,' he told her. 'You just saved a man's life tonight.'

Cathy smiled thinly. Now that she had had a chance to think, she realised the significance of what had occurred. The only man suspected of the murder of Betty Scott, apparently released by the police that day, had been left for dead in the road. Of course, it might have been a simple accident. After being freed, he might have celebrated with a good few too many beers and then stumbled into the path of a car. But why then hadn't the driver stopped to help him? She remembered the car that they had passed earlier, accelerating down the hill. Had the driver of this been the unintentional offender? The alternative was unspeakable, but it had to be faced. Had Thomas Hogg been mown down in cold blood? Cathy had doubted the poor man's guilt from the start. If the real killer of Betty Scott was still out there, they must be fearful of discovery and still it seemed, motivated to kill again.

## 23

Holly must have slept right through, because when she next awoke; it was seven o'clock in the morning and her mobile was reverberating on the bedside table. The screen lit up, indicating an unknown, local number. She answered, and the voice came like a faltering spasm.

'H-h-hello? Who is this I'm speaking to please?'

Holly felt like telling the unidentified caller that she was the one who had bloody well called, but instead, suddenly recognising the voice, she sat up very straight in bed. 'Marie? Is that you? What's the matter? What's happened?'

Holly could hear the old woman's breath at the end of the line, it came in shudders and it was obvious that she was struggling to speak.

'It's Thomas. Oh Goodness.' There was a long pause, during which Holly could hear her moving the receiver. And then her voice came again. 'Hello? Sorry, I'm at sixes and sevens. I'm sorry to call so early too, but I didn't know what else to do and you gave me your number, you see?'

'It's fine, Marie. What's happened to Thomas? He came

around here last night but I sent him away. He was drunk and in no fit state to be knocking on people's doors.'

'That makes sense. They couldn't understand why he'd been out of his house and especially in that weather.'

Getting out of bed with the phone still to her ear, Holly drew back the curtain and was met by a world that looked as if it had been brushed with a class A drug. The tops of the houses were completely covered, and she saw in the car park below, the inky tracks from cars that had already headed to work.

She waited, and eventually, it came. There had been an accident in one of the side-streets. It seemed that Thomas, whilst making his way home, had taken a minor detour. A motorist had found him lying. They had nearly run him over too but had managed to swerve. The man driving had helped him a good deal though. Marie said something about them having been in the emergency services or having knowledge of that sort of thing.

Holly found herself pacing the bedroom.

'Is he alright? What are his injuries?' she asked, knowing that the rapid-fire questions would do nothing to calm the poor woman who had broken the news.

'No, no, now don't you get in a panic as well,' she said, although the words sounded odd as she was so clearly in one herself. 'It's broken bones and he's punctured a lung. They've told me, he's going to be fine, but he'll be in for a few weeks I imagine, and pretty shaken by it all.'

'What was he doing?' Holly said as much to herself as Marie. 'He was drunk when he came. He even said he was going to die that night, and I told him off for coming. Now I feel terrible.'

'How were you to know it was going to happen?' she said. 'Thomas has been drunk many a time before this, and no doubt when he's discharged and back to his usual self, he'll be the same again. He's a law unto himself, that man.'

Holly could hear that she was both smiling and crying at the same time.

'What can I do?' Holly asked. 'Shall I pick you up? Do you want to go in to see him this morning?'

Poor Marie didn't need the worry at this time in her life. Thomas was no more than a rather awkward and unrewarding friend, and here she was, distraught over a man she owed nothing.

'You'll not be allowed in to see him outside visiting hours,' she said. 'They're strict like that. And I would know.'

'Well, this afternoon? I can get a taxi and we'll go together,' she said, wondering how in the name of God she would afford the fare. She sounded unsure, and Holly assumed that she'd misunderstood. 'Or maybe you'd like me to go for you?' she asked.

Marie made a satisfied sigh, and Holly knew that this had indeed been her intent. In many ways, it suited her better. She could catch the bus up there and not have to fork out more than a few pounds for the privilege.

'I've called the ward already this morning,' Marie said. 'It's thirty-two, orthopaedics.' She laughed again. 'I think he's already getting a name for himself,' she said.

'I'll bet,' Holly told her. She promised to send him her love and to keep in touch.

Having hung up, she sat on the edge of her bed for a good ten minutes thinking over what Marie had said. Poor, foolish Thomas. She could just imagine him flailing around all the way home, falling about the streets, shouting and carrying on. But why, she wondered, had he gone down some side-street? She imagined him staggering into the path of a car and his confusion and fear, knowing that he was painfully injured. At least, the driver had had the decency to stay with him.

Marie's words weren't lost on her though, and she had already wondered if the driver had been Alex, given that he had previously been in the emergency services. Perhaps it was all a little too coincidental. Had the accident been rather more deliberate, she wondered? Holly recalled Thomas's maddening final statement before he left her, and how he had said it loudly in a sing-song voice. He had said that he knew who had killed Betty. She imagined the drunken man floundering down the street, singing and laughing, as was his habit. Telling anyone who would listen, that he knew who the murderer was. Had that been the reason for his supposed accident? It certainly seemed possible.

Before anything else, she had to know if the driver had been Alex. She had ignored his message from the previous night, and now replied, asking if he had recovered fully from all the alcohol. She couldn't just go straight in and ask if he'd run over Thomas without sounding insane or at the very least, accusatory. Although she most desperately wanted an answer, Holly felt dismayed at the speed with which it came. It was just an overly cheery one-liner about him having had an early night the night before, but that was enough. Of course, he could have lied, but it certainly seemed from the message, that Alex wasn't in the frame for running people over anyway, and that to her, was a great relief.

The hospital told her two o'clock, but by the time her bus got in, it was a good bit after. She hung around the front of the ward waiting to speak with someone, but in the end, she gave up, and seeing his name on a big whiteboard, made her way to sideroom five.

He might well have just suffered a traumatic accident, but he was, at the very least, clean. It was the cleanest she had ever seen him, and even his teeth looked less yellow.

They had dressed him in one of their hospital gowns, printed with the name of the hospital in blue and yellow and green. A repetitive snake of words across his chest, shoulders and abdomen. When she entered the side-room, he was sleeping. His head was lolled back on the pillows. The oxygen mask had slipped, and the green, elastic cord that should have fitted snugly over his cheeks, had moved to his jaw, leaving the clear-plastic to sit awkwardly on the tip of his nose.

Holly sat down by the bed, not wanting to disturb him, not sure what she should say when he did wake. For a while, she listened to his rattled breathing. It felt almost voyeuristic to watch him as he rested. Holly wondered what she was doing there, and why she had come.

While she waited, she registered the pallor of his cheeks, the greying-yellow, wrinkled skin on his arms. She saw, to her surprise, that he had a tattoo on his right, upper arm. For some reason, this amused her. She found herself trying to decipher the faded, blue ink on his arm, but his skin was so sagged and creased that she couldn't make it out. She leaned in to get a better look, but couldn't tell what it was. His abdomen looked distended. Fat and round like a balloon. The covers on his bed rose up and over him in a tent-like fashion, clinging to his contours. She wondered if this was how he had always been. Perhaps his jacket had hidden it.

There was a tube coming out of his side; a chest drain. It had been fixed in place with what looked like duct-tape. The tube led to a container on the ground. Holly watched it for some time, as the bubbles came and went with each intake of his breath. She had no idea how long she sat.

When he awoke, it was with a jolt, and it obviously caused him some significant discomfort. The coughing seemed to wrack right through his body, all the way to his bones. She watched his chest heaving with the effort, fighting for gulps of air. His ribs sucked the fabric of the gown inwards, revealing his fragility. As he leaned forward, she saw his spine was a tangled cable, projecting gracelessly. His hands were flapping papers, grey and tremulous. She noticed only then, that one of his legs beneath the covers, was in plaster-cast also. Poor Thomas. He really had been in the wars.

Finally, he removed the oxygen mask, which had by this time, made its way to his chin and neck area, and clearly offered him little relief. His voice was croaky and it was an effort for him to force out the words. Holly watched his purple lips and the tongue darting to taste their cracked ridges.

'Told you,' he finally said, falling back on the pillows once more, utterly defeated by this exertion. But his eyes, although tired, watched keenly, and a smile twitched at the corners of his lips.

'You do like to cause a drama, don't you?' she asked.

The smile crept slyly upwards and played at the corners of his eyes, causing him to blink and involuntarily release a tear. She watched it travel the crevasses of his face. He raised a hand to wipe it away.

'Well, I must say, there are easier ways to get my attention. You heard that poor Marie was calling the hospital asking after you too, I suppose? Terribly upset, she's been.'

He didn't reply.

'What were you doing anyway?' she asked. 'I heard you were run over down a side-street in town. Where were you going?'

He shook his head sadly and then closed his eyes and she wondered if, in his exhausted state, he had fallen asleep. His breathing returned to some kind of normality. A rhythmical pattern, but the sound was all wrong. His chest rose and fell, bubbling and cracking with the struggle. Holly was almost as entranced by this, as his zip-running up and down. Up and down. Up and down.

She glanced around the room, wondering what they had done with his jacket, with the rest of his clothes. Probably put them in a plastic bag when he arrived here. Maybe they threw them in the bin or burned them. He probably had nothing other than the gown he was in now. She should have brought him clothes, a toothbrush. Wasn't that what visitors did? At least his beloved bag on wheels was still by his bed. Holly smiled. They'd clearly not managed to confiscate that.

His eyelids fluttered and he squinted at the overhead striplight. It was an unflattering glare at the best of times, but it only served to enhance his sallowness. The fissures of his skin gaped and fractured, showing deep shadows and hollows where they should not be. In the open air, standing before her in the street, he had never looked this way. He was like a different person now. Older, and far sadder.

He shifted in the bed, moving his good leg beneath the covers and projecting his frail body into another spasm of coughing. Again, she waited for it to pass, not moving to offer him misguided help. Finally, he looked at her with undeniable mischief, and she saw that although in physical appearance he had altered, in character he was, thankfully, still just the same.

It came like a whisper. His eyes spoke it before his lips. 'Eight. I was right. It was my number all along. My time,' he mouthed. 'Told you I was going to die.' After he had spoken, he seemed slightly bolstered. His bony hands reached behind him, finding some holding on the mattress. He pushed his weight backwards, shuffling so that he was sitting more upright. A low cawing chuckle exuded his being. His shoulders shook with the force of it.

'No one else would find it funny, you know? You've just been run over. It wasn't your time though, and you didn't die. I assume this was up by Fernibanks?' she asked, in mock-annoyance.

For all of his silliness, Thomas knew when to conserve his energy and instead of answering, he simply nodded and smiled.

'You're safe here,' she said, and he closed his eyes in assent.

He had been going to the old psychiatric hospital. Of course. Everything seemed to lead back there.

## 24

Holly left the hospital not long after. Taking the bus back into town, she got off a good ten stops before her flat so that she could go in to speak to Marie. The roads were reasonably busy, with commuters perhaps chancing an early finish and heading home. The pavements, although gritted, were slushy in places and where footfall had not been, there was still a mat of thin snow. A good hour's rain and the lot would be gone. Holly imagined the delight of children waking to the white-out that morning, but for Marie, and some of the other less mobile individuals, it might result in days being housebound.

As usual, Marie had seen her coming. Holly supposed that she spent much of her day poised by the window, perhaps hoping for visitors. She walked up the front path, following a line of paw prints, presumably belonging to the persistent cat that had once belonged to Betty but had long since adopted Marie. The door opened and she greeted Holly like an old friend, ushering her inside with the offer this time, of tea.

'Well,' she said. 'How is he? I called again at lunchtime and they told me he was sleeping.'

'Probably sleeping off the hangover,' Holly laughed. 'No, he's alright, honestly. He was in very good spirits. Well, you can imagine, what with all the attention.'

Marie shook her head fondly. 'He's some boy, that one.'

Once Marie had faffed around in the kitchen a good deal and then finally settled herself in one of the chairs, Holly felt able to speak more freely. She wasn't quite sure how the other woman was going to take what she was about to tell her, but the thought of mentioning it as she carried a boiling mug of tea, didn't seem such a good idea.

When Holly told her that she suspected Thomas's accident had not been accidental, she was glad that she hadn't just blurted it out. The old woman's hands trembled and she covered one with the other in an attempt to stop the motion.

'He's too exhausted to speak at length,' Holly told her. 'Do you think you'd be able to fill in some gaps for me?'

Marie nodded.

If only they had had the conversation before all this mess, but Holly had not known the direction things might take.

'Thomas has lived in this town for most of his life,' Holly began.

'He has,' Marie agreed. 'He went to school here. It wasn't a great success to be fair, from what he's told me. He should have gone to one of those special schools. They do wonders with disabled children these days. But poor Thomas must have found himself quite lost in a regular school.'

'And the butt of a good many jokes too, I imagine,' Holly said. 'Having a lower than average intellect, no matter how genuine and charming he was, it must have been difficult. He still can't read, am I right?'

'Yes, that's right. Good with his numbers and ever so proud of that, he is, but words, no. He talked about it with me right back at the start. I think it wasn't only the school kids either, although they can be so cruel, can't they? No, it was the teachers as well. I think he was given the belt for next-to-nothing, and probably almost daily too. Poor little boy, he must have been. It's a wonder he doesn't hate folk given what he's had in the past.'

Holly could tell it hurt her to consider her friend in any pain at all, no matter how long ago it had been.

'I know I'm jumping around a bit, Marie,' she apologised, 'but bear with me. Both you and Thomas will have been in this town for most of your lives then? And this would have been back when Thomas was only a boy, but perhaps you'll remember better. I wonder, do you recollect the fire up at the old psychiatric hospital?'

Marie looked surprised. 'Now, that's a while back, but yes, I remember, of course. It was the talk of the town for a long time, and the newspaper people were everywhere, taking photos and asking questions. Not that they got much, I don't suppose. I was married then, but not working. I don't recall the details of the fire. Back then, the town was quite different.'

'A man died,' Holly said. She watched the old woman shake her head sadly.

'There was no suspicion of anyone else being involved though, from what I remember. It was a horrible thing all the same. Just a dreadful accident. The police looked for witnesses I'm sure, in the beginning, but I think it was assumed that the doctor had been up in the building and had possibly been smoking. They really shouldn't have, even back then because of the oxygen being so flammable. Anyway, after that, the place started to close down. It was more of a mental home than a mental hospital. Quite outdated really and closing it was long overdue. Some people had been in there for far too many years. They'd never put folk like that in hospital these days. That's what I remember anyway.'

'I see,' Holly said. 'Was Thomas in the hospital ever?'

'Oh no,' the old woman said without hesitation. 'Not that I knew of anyway. His mother was, I believe. She was a poor crater. Very sad. I suppose he went up to visit when he was very young, but she was no use to him. It probably only confused him going to see her.'

'And Betty?'

'Well, you already know she was matron up there for a good number of years. Very strict, but good at her job. Fair, if you know what I mean?'

Holly nodded.

'Marie,' she said. 'I think that Betty's death had something to do with the fire at the old psychiatric hospital.' Holly looked out of the window at the house opposite where Betty had lived. When she spoke again, it was more to herself than Marie. 'But I'm still struggling to make the connection. I know that they are linked, without a doubt, but how? The fire. Was it deliberately set?'

Marie rested back in her chair. 'And you said before, that you think the same person might have purposely run over Thomas last night? Do you think they wanted to kill him then?'

'It's a bit of a coincidence, isn't it?' Holly said. 'He'd been singing and shouting up and down the streets about knowing who killed Betty. Then he gets hit by a car.'

'And does he?' Marie asked. 'Does he really know who it was?'

'It was all just drunken talk. I asked him if he thought he'd been targeted, and he couldn't say. Just told me he knew it was his time to die. He's obsessed with time and numbers, isn't he?'

'He's always been that way, ever since I remember,' Marie said. 'He's like a magpie for times and dates and so on. If he ever lets you look inside his bag, you'll see them all. Scraps of paper with jotted down notes of numbers. He must have been collecting them for years and years. You care about him, don't you?' she asked.

Holly felt her cheeks redden. Perhaps in Thomas, she had recognised a fellow outcast. Maybe the unfairness of his treatment reminded her of herself. It was ironic, given how many lies she told herself, but justice was important. 'You always back the underdog,' her mother had once commented. At the time, Holly hadn't understood, but now she was older, she knew why.

Marie made a bit of a fuss when she said she was leaving. She insisted on her taking away a homemade steak pie and a cherry cake. The old woman said that she needed feeding up. Holly wondered if she had ever had children of her own. There were no photographs of toothy grandchildren. Sad, Holly thought, given how maternal the woman was. She took the offerings, balancing the two dishes as she closed the old lady's door. She supposed that she must have looked a bit of a state, for Marie to offer them to her. All the same, she knew that she couldn't stomach food that night.

Having left the house, Holly made her way back along the street. The cars and their headlights came and went. Her feet beat a well-trodden path. The high street was chaotic, as shoppers and people rushing home from work, darted in and out of doorways. Car doors opened and slammed shut, and the swish of tyres on mud-spattered gutters came and went.

For the life of her, she still couldn't understand the connection between Betty's killer and the tragedy at the old hospital all those years ago. Of course, she had assumed that the fire had been an accident. What if it really had been a deliberate fire? What if, rather than allowing the psychiatrist to perish, someone had deliberately lured him there? Holly recalled Neil's words. 'They all close ranks,' he had said of the doctors. Holly doubted if an entire group of skilled professionals could turn their backs. She sighed. Had Betty been the killer? Had she locked the psychiatrist in the building and allowed him to die? Was that why she was murdered, out of revenge? But why would Betty do such a thing?

Betty had been such an odd person in many ways; secretive and manipulative in her day-to-day dealings with people, even as an old woman. Holly thought of all of the people who had disliked her, and all of the reasons they had to do so. She recalled her dogmatic approach in dealing with Carol and Tricia over the till. Then there was Neil, and even Alex, who Holly suspected had been the recipient of her mild intimidation, or at worst, blackmail. Neil, for his immoral practices in selling on charitable donations for great profit, and Alex, for his murky motives in leaving his job. Without the hospital fire even being part of it, they all had a reason to dislike or even fear the old woman. Even she, Holly. Perhaps she had a greater reason than them all.

## 25

'Good morning,' Cathy said, entering the charity shop. The woman behind the front desk seemed flustered. She had a spiral notebook in front of her and appeared to have been crossing something out. She pushed this to the side and turned to smile.

'Oh hello, can I help?'

'I was hoping to speak to someone about fundraising, and to offer mine, well, our, services, in a way. I'm Dr Moreland from the medical practice up the road. Elizabeth Scott was my patient and before she died, she had come in and asked me to help. I thought, out of respect I might ...'

'Well, how kind,' the woman said. She clapped her hands together in delight. 'Tricia,' she called, and from the back of the shop, another woman of more substantial and determined proportions appeared.

'Carol?' the other woman asked. 'Anything up?'

'Yes, look who's come to help! A doctor from the surgery. We haven't had the pleasure,' she waffled.

Cathy smiled. Perhaps she was making a big mistake coming here, but she couldn't just sit and do nothing. She'd called the police that morning. All in hand, they had reassured her. Yes, they'd heard about Mr Hogg's misfortune. 'A little more than misfortune,' Cathy had said but she could tell by the tone of his voice, that the police officer was getting annoyed. 'If you'd just leave us to do our job, Doctor,' he had said. 'I'm sure we'd get things done a lot faster.'

'So, Betty had been in and asked before she died, had she? She never told us, did she Tricia?' the woman said, grinning and nodding at her assistant. 'And I was crossing out her name in the book just now, going through all the days she'd put herself down to work too. Terribly sad. But now the doctor's come to offer to help and what a blessing that will be. Was it the tombola that Betty mentioned? We've had a good number of donations but we were hoping for a big turnover this year. We're trying to make it our best yet,' she explained. 'The charity shop's takings go centrally, you see? The little fundraisers that we do in our own time, under the charity name, are for us. Well, not us personally, of course,' she laughed. 'Our locality, you see? That's why it's so vital we do well.'

'And Betty came in and asked?' the woman called Tricia enquired again.

'Well, she was seeing me anyway, but yes, she said she wanted help.' Cathy smiled. 'Perhaps if I asked at the surgery? Maybe the other staff? What kind of donations are you looking for? Booze? Gifts? That sort of thing?'

Carol was nodding enthusiastically. 'Oh yes, anything of that sort. Nothing too ordinary, if you see what I mean? I was going to be cheeky and ask, but I'm afraid you might say no …'

Cathy waited.

'Well, seeing as you're here, I might as well ask. It's probably against the rules, but might you find a little place to put up a few posters? I know that you can't show interest in a particular charity really, but seeing as it was Betty who asked in the first place ...'

'I don't know ...' Cathy began.

'Out of respect for the old lady,' Carol continued, her eyes flashing with enthusiasm. 'It would be a nice tribute.' She moved the A4 notebook to the side and reached below the front desk. Before Cathy could refuse, she was unravelling a tube of printouts.

Cathy felt sick. 'Alright,' she said. 'I'll see what I can do with them. We don't usually, as a rule.'

Carol clapped her hands together again in delight. 'Well, there you go, and I thought you'd refuse. How wonderful. Isn't it wonderful, Tricia? We've been wracking our brains over how to get the word out there, and the surgery has such heavy footfall. Of course, the fundraising's all rather fallen by the wayside what with poor Betty's death and the investigation.'

Cathy nodded. 'Yes, I am sorry. It must have been a shock. Had she worked here a long time then?'

'Before I started, and you Tricia, wasn't it?' Carol said.

'She used to be a nurse; I believe?' Cathy asked.

'Oh, a long time ago that was, of course. Poor Betty. No, she was fairly getting on,'

Cathy smiled. 'But still very much all there,'

'True enough,' Carol said. 'Although sometimes she got muddled. Not the easiest to work with though, as you might imagine. Stuck in her ways.'

Tricia nodded in agreement.

Cathy saw a man now hovering through by the back door. Carol must have seen also because she called to him. 'Neil, come through and get Alex and Holly. This is the doctor from up the road. She's offering to help with the tombola.'

From the back of the shop, the man who Cathy now knew

was Neil, approached. She thought she recognised him, but couldn't recall having seen him professionally recently.

'Alright Doc?' he asked, and Cathy smiled and nodded.

Behind him, she saw a young woman emerge, closely followed by another man. Before Cathy could stop herself, she gasped.

The man looked just as dumbfounded.

'Alex?' she said in disbelief, and then smiling, she shook her head. 'You won't remember me, probably, will you?' she said. 'I'm an old friend of Sally's from med school. I've only just seen her a couple of weeks ago too. A reunion dinner.'

'My God,' the man said as he came out into the shop.

Cathy thought the young woman beside him looked irritated, and she wondered why, but Alex was looking her up and down now and smiling.

'So, you stayed in the area after leaving medical school, did you?' Alex asked. 'And how are you, Cathy? I remember you, of course. I can't believe it. It must be near enough ten years. You look fine. Are you well?'

By now, the group of volunteers were looking on in amazement.

'We should meet up sometime,' Alex said, glancing around.

'Sure. Yes,' Cathy said. 'That would be good. I came in to offer help. I certainly didn't expect to find you here.'

'Long story,' Alex said. He looked at the young woman behind him, and Cathy wondered how the two of them were connected.

'Well, I had better go. Nice to see you, Alex,' she said, feeling that the mood in the shop had changed somewhat since she had first come in. 'Here's my number if you're free for a coffee. I was asking Sally after you. I wondered; you see?'

'Yes, I see,' Alex said, and his cheeks reddened.

'Nice to meet you all,' Cathy said.

But Carol wasn't finished. 'Before you go,' she said, leaning across the desk. 'Here. If you're a member of the team and helping us out, you'd better wear this.' She held out a ribbon, with a pin attached to the back. 'It's for the charity,' the woman explained.

'Oh, thanks,' Cathy said, now desperate to leave. She took the pin badge and slipping it into her pocket, left.

She spent all that day thinking about her visit to the charity shop and her surprise discovery there. Suzalinna was correct. She had always had rather a thing for Alex when he was dating Sally and if anything, age had only served to improve him.

Arriving home after work, she forced herself to consider the rest of the volunteers in turn. That had been the real reason for her visit, after all. Carol, it seemed, was the principal helper. Cathy paused as she poured herself a mug of tea. She stirred the teabag around and around, watching as the liquid darkened. She carried her drink through to the living room and sat down. Was Carol in the frame then? The over-anxious do-gooder; could she be a potential murderer? It all seemed unlikely, but then Betty's death and the possible attempted murder of Thomas Hogg were just as outlandish.

Cathy had called the hospital twice that day to ask after the man. He had been in theatre the first time she had rung, apparently having his leg re-positioned as the fracture was unstable. Cathy had been more concerned about his neck and back, but the senior registrar that she spoke to said that Thomas had been lucky. He laughed about the pen trick she had used to treat the tension pneumothorax and told her that the A and E staff had been quite surprised when Thomas had come in. The talk of the hospital, it had been that evening. Cathy hung up feeling reassured. At least, it seemed, Thomas was safe for now.

Cathy knew that Betty had believed there was danger in the charity shop, and the answer to her death must surely lie there.

It helped of course, that she now had a reason to speak to the volunteers with the silly tombola to assist with. Cathy wondered if this had been Betty's plan all along. Had the old woman, cunningly given her a route in? Perhaps she had hoped that Cathy too, might see the potentially alarming individual and, as a doctor, spot the signs and know what to do.

Nothing had sprung out at her though when she had visited. The woman Tricia was vaguely familiar, as was the older man who had come through the shop. Neil, she thought Carol had called him. They were possibly patients, but she couldn't recall seeing them recently anyway. She definitely hadn't seen the po-faced younger woman before. Cathy had forgotten what she had been called. Pretty, she thought, but without a doubt, brooding. Of all of the volunteers, it was she who looked the most out of place.

Cathy knew that the best way to find out everyone's story was through Alex, although she hated to pump him for inside information. It was, however, an excellent opportunity to reacquaint herself with him. And Cathy did not have to wait long before she received the call. The unknown number flashed up on her mobile screen later that evening. The noise cut through the stillness of her own home, making her jump. She snatched up her phone and had to stop herself from answering on the second ring.

When she heard Alex's voice, though, she relaxed and laughed at her eagerness.

'Cathy? Thank God you didn't give me a false number. I wondered if you really wanted to catch up or if you were just being polite.'

Alex, as she remembered, had never been one to play games. He had been straight with Sally the whole time they had been dating. He had treated her well, as far as Cathy could remember, often going out of his way to fit around her revision schedules or hospital placements, so that they could spend more time together. He had been working himself. A young police officer, back then. Cathy thought that Sally and he had met in a club on a night out. Probably during a medic pub crawl. There had been plenty of those. He had become a regular fixture on the medical scene, coming to dances and evenings out, and had even been given the honorary title 'Dr Plod' by one of Cathy's friends. He was always the sober one, the voice of reason, and guaranteed to get them safely home at the end of the night.

'We should meet up,' Cathy said simply, and he agreed that they should.

'Is tomorrow too keen?'

Cathy smiled and tried not to sound too pleased.

When she hung up, having agreed on the specifics, she forced herself to remember that she was trying to find justice for Betty Scott and Thomas Hogg, not acquire a new love interest. Alex, after all, worked in the charity shop. It was an uncomfortable thought, but it put him as much in the frame as the rest of them.

## 26

Having woken early and eaten her way through Marie's generous offerings that up until then, she had forgotten about, Holly returned to the charity shop with renewed determination. She knew now that the only thing for it was to find physical evidence. Thomas at least was safe in the hospital. The quicker she got to the bottom of things now, the better. The police had been in again, and it seemed that the blood found at The Court outside Thomas's flats was definitely Betty's. They spoke to Tricia for a while in private. Holly supposed it was because the silly woman had told them that she visited one of the pensioners up in The Court regularly. It was just one of her good deeds. Holly didn't suppose the police distrusted her, but they probably wanted to see if she had seen anything suspicious while she was there.

Holly had thought a good deal about the state of play. Until the police found something concrete, she felt that Thomas was still very much in the frame, despite his recent accident, which she assumed the police believed to be just that. She knew that the evidence could lie nowhere other than in one place. But how would she pull the damn thing off?

In the end, she decided on a story.

'Heavens,' Carol said with real concern when she told her. 'When were you last wearing it, then?'

Holly screwed up her face as if she was trying hard to think. She had already flushed her cheeks by slapping them in the toilet cubicle, to appear thoroughly distressed. She had even gone to the trouble of splashing tap water into her eyes until they stung. When Holly observed herself dispassionately in the mirror, she did look the part.

They were standing by the till, and thankfully Tricia wasn't around. A customer hurriedly paid for their goods and then withdrew leaving them to have, what must appear to be, an upsetting discussion.

'That's just it, Carol. I can't remember. I've already gone over my flat last night and I've been up and down the street too looking, but the shop is the only place it can be.' She pretended to think again. 'I definitely had it on when I was sorting the stuff for the skip.'

Carol looked like she knew something but she didn't have the heart to say. 'Well, we can all have a good look now, if you like. What did you say it was like?'

Holly described some hideous, overelaborate, gold ring. To add to the drama, she gave it a small sapphire surrounded by diamonds, just to make it sound like a worthwhile search.

'It was my grandmother's, you see?' Holly said to her, wiping her forehead with her sleeve. 'Although the monetary value isn't great, it's the sentiment, you see?'

Carol, always ready to show her magnanimous side, patted Holly on the arm. 'We'll find it today. Don't you worry.' But Holly knew that Carol didn't believe her own words.

Even Tricia dropped her scroll of labels to join in the search. She went so far as to get down on her hands and knees and look behind the toilet bowl, an act that Holly thought went way above and beyond the call of duty. Alex said that he was sure he had seen some nice jewellery coming in the other week, and both he and Neil searched to see if it had been accidentally placed with that, but it seemed that it all been sold, as these glass, sparkly items often were. In the end, after an hour of fruitless and frankly, overacted hunting on Holly's part, Carol finally said that they'd have to give it up. Holly put up a bit of a fight, saying that maybe if they just looked a bit harder, but Carol would have none of it.

'I didn't want to say it at the start,' she said, 'but when you told me that you had been sorting things for the skip, it did cross my mind ...'

Holly stared at her. 'What, Carol?' she asked, forcing the older woman to break the bad news.

'Well, there's always the chance that it fell off into the skip if you were throwing bags over the side the other day. I'm sorry, I didn't want to say, but ...'

Holly did her best impression of someone hearing a devastating truth. She really went to town and enjoyed herself.

'Of course,' she said. 'How could I have been so stupid? I'll have to look.' This, she said vehemently, as if her life depended on it.

When she had made herself plain, Carol looked utterly incredulous. 'You can't,' she stammered. 'It's impossible. It would be like looking for a needle in a haystack. Imagine the mess too.'

Holly stayed firm though. Health and safety were thrown into the mix of obstructions by Carol, but still, she wouldn't be turned. Holly could see that it bothered Carol a good deal and she wondered why. Did she have something to hide after all? Had she thrown something in the skip that perhaps she shouldn't? If anything, it made Holly outrageously determined, and she could see that Carol knew it too.

'I'll begin after lunch if that's alright?' Holly said. 'I think we have enough people in the shop today anyway, so I'm surplus. I've probably caused everyone enough trouble as it is this morning.'

Carol didn't disagree.

Holly had brought in a backpack from home, with a set of overalls. She changed into them in the toilet while the others stood drinking their tea. She quickly grabbed her own proffered mug as she passed, and drank the lukewarm liquid. God alone knew how she would ever eat or drink again after rummaging around the skip.

Walking through the shop, she snapped on a pair of disposable gloves. After a second thought, Holly double-gloved to be extra safe, and went out, around the side of the building to the yellow cavernous pit, which was beginning to look far less cavernous than when she had last been there. It appeared that the rest of the team had been busily slinging bag after bag into the wretched metal box.

It wasn't easy to get into the damn thing, but once Holly had finally managed to clamber up, hauling herself over the cold side, bruising her ribs in the process, she stood, her feet sinking into the binbags. The smell was atrocious, which was surprising, given that the majority of the contents must only be clothes, but when she came across a bag full of food waste, she began to get edgy about rats. A wave of nausea suddenly hit her and the saliva in her mouth pooled. She shook her head in annoyance.

She began to move gingerly about, coming across an arch-enemy almost immediately. She had grazed her ankles on the damn thing while it sat in the shop, unwanted. The multi-coloured plastic emerged and she lifted the horrible cat basket and flung it to the side. Due to the freezing weather overnight, the plastic, on hitting metal, shattered, a glorious smash of fragments. It almost made up for the arduous job with which she had encumbered herself.

Being of a scientific mind, Holly did things methodically. She started at one end and then threw the bags that she had already opened over to the right, piling them high to make more room. A couple of passersby stopped and shouted something. Holly guessed that they worked for the garage on the other side of the car park, but she ignored them, not seeing any reason to explain herself. She must have looked quite a sight. Numerous opened bags brought back a recollection of why they had been discarded in the first place. Some of the clothes were stained and some even torn. Some were covered in dog hair or so worn that they would be impossible to sell. Some were of the variety that they could not sell anyway for hygiene reasons; the pyjamas, the underwear, she raked through it all.

After twenty minutes of searching, she stood up and rested. It was hard going, repeatedly bending down and throwing. Many were now damp from being left out overnight. The front of her overalls was stained and wet, the disposable gloves were ripped at the wrist and inside them, her hands sweated, despite the cold. Her limbs felt heavy and useless.

Neil appeared at that point, clearly keen to caw over her when she was at her most vulnerable.

'Still not found it?' he asked.

He had put on his overcoat to come around and brought with him a steaming mug. Holly stood still panting, her hair loose in strands now over her face.

'Nothing yet,' she told him, blowing her hair off her forehead. 'I'm not giving up though.'

'Brought you a cup of tea to warm your hands,' he said. 'Don't suppose you'll find the ring though. Sounded like something I had in at the shop years ago. Nice, it was too, and pricey.'

Holly ignored the proffered mug. How in the name of God could she stand in a skip and sip a cup of bloody tea anyway?

'I'd better get back to it,' she said, turning her back on him. She hoped that he wasn't going to stand and watch. If he did, her search would have to be far more thorough for his benefit. 'Go inside,' she called over her shoulder. 'There's no point in both of us getting cold.'

She didn't turn to see but heard his footsteps retreating. Relieved to be alone once more, she continued. The only window looking out onto the car park from the charity shop was the one belonging to the toilet. Several times, she was aware of the light going on and off again, but the glass was frosted to protect the user's modesty. Holly wondered if they were trying to peer through the hazed window to see how she was getting on, but she was too busy to bother.

In the end, she came close to the middle of the skip and felt sure that if luck was on her side, she'd be granted the long-awaited bag. Several times, she had half fallen as she clambered over things, and had already had to grab out to the side once, catching hold of a broken mirror and scratching her arm. Holly hoped to goodness that it wasn't going to be in vain, after everything she had been through that day.

After another ten minutes and almost despairing by that point, she finally found what she was looking for. It was funny because as soon as she touched the black refuse sack, she knew that it was the one. She hardly dared believe it though and tentatively untied the knot. Inside was the second bag, as Holly knew it must be. It was her who had placed it there the week or so before, after all. It took all of her will-power not to rip the bag open and allow the contents to spill forth, but she knew that the police would need to see it and there were ways of doing these things.

The murderer had known what they were doing. They knew

that whoever sorted through this bag would be unwilling to fully open it if it were wet, and this indicated to Holly that it had been either one of the charity shop workers or a regular customer. It had to be. Only insider knowledge would allow for this. They had, she assumed, thought it possible that the police might be suspicious and begin to search through personal bins looking for the clothes worn to kill Betty, as they had clearly already done in Thomas's case. What safer place to get rid of the bloodstained clothes than the charity shop? And even better, the bag would now have any number of fingerprints on it. Far more sensible to leave it for one of the volunteers to handle, rather than tossing it directly into the skip themselves. And the irony must not have been lost on the perpetrator, who knew full-well that the evidence lay safely behind the very shop in which they had worked alongside their victim. Holly wondered at their audacity, but to murder someone must, in itself, take some daring. And who would question a donation?

Holly recalled that day, opening up the shop with Carol, and together, them pulling the bags through. They had been piled high at the front door and Holly remembered having to dash through to the back carrying this one as it had leaked a trail of brown. Carol had had to bleach the floor again afterwards.

Slowly, Holly reached into the sack. The boots were the first thing that she touched. She pushed her hand in further and touched the damp fabric. She was almost too afraid to pull the clothing out, knowing that the garment must surely be streaked with the blood of the old woman who she had once worked alongside.

The rain had started to come on. It fell in an icy drizzle, but Holly hardly noticed. She didn't know how she was going to explain her discovery to the rest of the volunteers, but the police would most certainly have to be informed, and as soon as possible.

# 27

Holly was frozen, her body shaking uncontrollably. Whether it was because of the dreadful discovery or the cold, she didn't know. She realised that she would have to go inside first and clean up before informing the police. She left the bag in the skip, not wanting to disturb the evidence any further than necessary and somehow, slung her body over the side.

'Any luck?' Carol asked, standing at the till, with the electric heater on full blast.

Holly shook her head. It hurt to look at the strip lighting. Her wearisome feet were no act this time. Holly walked through to the back. She passed Alex who asked her the same, but before she even told him, he must have known.

'Cheer up. I bet it's at home after all,' he said. 'I'll check my house if you want. Were you wearing it that night, by the way?'

Unfortunately, Neil appeared in the doorway at that point. Having clearly overheard, he looked from Alex to her, shaking his head, and all the time grinning like some inane chimp.

''A Charitable Romance.' It has a ring to it, no Alex? One of those trashy novels that we get in.' He made as to jog Alex's arm, but missed and flailed his elbow in mid-air.

Alex laughed it off, but she was too troubled to even try to feign amusement. She continued through to the toilet and shut the door, locking herself in. She sat on the covered seat, not needing to use the lavatory, but welcoming the solitude. Outside, she heard the muffled voices of the two men, with Neil's jovial banter impossible to ignore, even though the words were no longer fully audible. The tiny room was draughty, and the bars on the small, frosted window made it feel like a cell. Carol had tried to brighten things up with heart-shaped soaps laid out on the cistern, and a rose-scented air-freshener.

Holly sat there trembling, her head bowed, the heels of her hands pushed deep into her eye sockets, willing herself to think. Where she went from here, she didn't know. She had now found physical evidence implicating a charity shop volunteer. She had achieved what she set out to do. Why then, did she baulk at the thought of informing the police?

There was a tap at the door which made her jump.

'Holly?' came Alex's voice. 'I've made you a hot coffee. Come out and drink it, please. You must be frozen.'

'Just coming,' she called, and listened to him pause, and then, she heard his footsteps retreat.

Holly leaned her head against the cold woodchip of the wall, feeling the pattern like hives against her skin. Although she had been frozen through, she was sweating. She needed to take stock, and change direction. She would inform the police and begin to think again. Someone in the shop must have had a strong motive to kill. It was odd how much it bothered her, but it did. Perhaps she was fonder of them than she had made out. How might she feel if it turned out to be one of the volunteers? But if she was serious about solving the damn thing, and for some reason, she had assigned herself the task now, she must be prepared for what was to come.

It seemed to Holly, that the only way to get to the bottom of all of this, was to find a real and substantial motive. Without that, anyone or his neighbour might have murdered Betty. Finding irrefutable and strong motivation for the murder must be the only way forward. If she knew why the crime had been committed, it had to lead to the perpetrator. The police could run their lab tests and comb the clothing in the skip for DNA, or whatever. Holly knew, though, that the evidence might not be enough in court, as any one of the volunteers might have good reason to have DNA on the damn garments given that they had come through the shop.

Holly finally unlocked the door having freshened up, she walked back through.

'Thanks,' she said and downed the mug of coffee that Alex had left her on the side. 'I need to make a phone call. Back in a bit.' She made her way to the door. 'I just need to nip out. Private call,' she explained to Carol who raised her eyebrows.

Not knowing who she should ask to speak to, Holly stood on the doorstep, scrolling down through her phone. It was hardly a nine-nine-nine call of course. She yawned and leaned back on the shop window. The day seemed to have gone on forever. Her head felt fuzzy and ached. Holly looked down at her phone screen. The numbers seemed to be moving. She took a step forward and held the phone out at arm's length. Stupid bloody thing. Still, it wasn't right. She looked across the street and saw people looking across at her and pointing. The sound of the traffic was muffled and low. She shook her head, trying to clear it. What was wrong with her? And then, the picture distorted and changed angle. She saw feet and ankles, and then nothing.

## 28

'Cathy? It's Alex. Can you talk?'

He sounded breathless, and Cathy could hear traffic in the background.

'I'm about to call in a patient, Alex, what's up?' she asked, glancing at her computer screen.

It was only the following day, and they had already arranged a time to meet up later that evening. If Cathy was honest, she was a little hashed. It had been a busy morning already and she had slept little the night before for worrying about Betty's death.

Alex's voice was emotionless. 'It's fine, I'll call nine-nine-nine,' he said. The phone went dead.

Cathy paced up and down her room as she repeatedly tried to call him back, but instead of hearing his voice, she got the engaged signal. She swore under her breath and phoned through to Michelle.

'Michelle? I've only got two booked-in as duty doctor, can you transfer both to Linda, I see she's quiet? I've just had an emergency call. I need to go out.'

'Of course, Dr Moreland. They didn't come through us though, was the call direct to you?'

'Yes, I gave out my mobile number. I'll have to go. Apologise to Linda for me, please. I'm not sure how long I'll be.'

Cathy took her doctors' bag, not knowing if she might need it. She snatched up her car keys and jogged down the corridor to the back door. All the while, her mind was racing. She assumed that Alex must be at the charity shop given the time of day, but she had no idea really. It could end up being a wild goose chase, but by the tone of his voice, something awful had happened. Getting into her car, she signalled left and turned out of the practice car park, heading into town. The rain had come on and was now falling quite heavily in icy sheets. The roads were treacherous. Twice her traction control kicked in, juddering the car as she turned too tight around a corner. What on earth was going on? Why had he said he'd need to call the emergency services? Had someone else been hurt, and if so, who?

She saw them long before she was anywhere near the charity shop. Blue lights lit up the neighbouring buildings, sending fierce, fluorescent lightning into the already charged atmosphere. The ambulance had parked up and was blocking half of the road, meaning the cars were gridlocked. Cathy abandoned her own down a side-street and ran up towards the shop carrying her doctors' bag. When she arrived though, the ambulance crew were already shutting the doors and getting in the cab.

She saw Alex then. He looked dreadful. His face was pale and he ran his hand around the back of his neck.

'What happened?' she asked, going to him.

He shook his head, clearly in shock. 'It was Holly. I don't know what happened. She went out to make a phone call and then someone on the street came crashing in the shop saying she had collapsed. She looked horrible, Cathy. The ambulance crew put an intravenous line in her and said they'd just take her straight in.'

Cathy saw the rest of the volunteers peering out from inside the shop.

'What did the paramedics think it was?' Cathy asked.

Alex finally met her gaze, having watched the ambulance reverse and then move away. His eyes were a cool grey. 'Cathy, I don't want to be over the top, and I didn't want to say it to them, but I think she's got a very serious drink problem.'

Cathy stared at him. 'Oh?'

'She was fine today though. She's been buzzing around the place all morning, to be fair. I've known for a while that she drinks too much. It's been obvious since she started working here three or four months ago. She'd come in half-cut some days, not that the rest of them probably noticed. Stinking of it. She's been at my place too. Arrived with bottles of vodka. Very troubled girl. Honestly, I don't know what brought her to Glainkirk in the first place. She's like a fish out of water. Incredibly smart. None of us knows a thing about her. I liked her though. There was something candid. Innocent, I suppose, although she could be a brat.'

'You're talking in the past tense.'

Alex smiled slightly. 'You always were sharp, Cathy. I'm so glad that you turned up again. Slip of the tongue. I hope she'll be fine. She's young after all, only in her twenties. Whatever is wrong with her, at least she has age on her side.'

Cathy nodded. 'So, she just arrived in Glainkirk a few months ago?'

'Yes,' Alex said, now looking calmer. 'She was a feisty little menace at times. Caused mayhem in the shop and irritated the hell out of Carol, purely out of devilment, it seemed. Carol won't miss her while she's in hospital, that's for sure, nor will Tricia, for that matter. Always winding them up.'

'How was she with Betty?' Cathy asked, not knowing quite why she did so.

Alex looked at her thoughtfully. 'Funny,' he said, folding his arms. 'She took it quite badly; Betty's death, as it happens. Adopted almost a vigilante role really, trying to find out what had caused the old woman's death. That was why she turned up at my door. Wanted to thrash out some ideas about who might have been the culprit.'

'And who did she suspect?' Cathy asked, hardly daring to breathe.

'Oh, just about everyone in the shop, but then she was like that. She had a good imagination and could come up with a tale to fit all of them. She will have no doubt suspected me too, I imagine.' Alex laughed. 'It got far worse, I suppose, after Neil's story about Fernibanks just before Christmas. She was sure that it linked back to the old hospital and the tragedy up there.'

'Alex,' Cathy said seriously. 'We need to talk about this. About all of it. What was she doing before she fell ill today?'

He laughed, but his eyes didn't smile. 'Rummaging around in the skip out the back. Said she'd lost a ring, although I must say, I never saw her wearing one.'

Cathy raised her eyebrows but didn't comment. 'Are you still OK to meet up later?' she said instead. 'I need to get back to the surgery just now. I flew out of the place with no explanation.'

Alex nodded. 'Thanks, Cathy. I appreciate ... Well, you know.'

∼

BETWEEN PATIENTS, she rang up A and E to enquire after the girl Holly. It was Suzalinna's senior registrar who spoke with her, a man called Brodie who she had met a couple of times on nights out with her friend.

'What do you think then?' she asked. 'I have heard that she is a heavy drinker, but other than that, she's not bothered to register with the practice since moving to the area approximately four months ago. She was a volunteer at the charity shop and lived alone, but that's about all I know. I'll be speaking with someone who may have known her more intimately later on, so I'll ask him about her history.'

'We suspected from her lab results that alcohol was an issue. It explains the deranged liver function, No, it's renal function that's worrying us though, Cathy. I'm getting her transferred up to the unit in the next hour if she goes off any more. She's acidotic. Very.'

'Do you think she's taken something?'

'She's drifting in and out. Very sedated. Yes, that's my suspicion. Overdose. You know how long the poisons stuff takes to come back though. We'll treat her symptomatically until we know. Her temperature's high, and when she arrived, she was in sinus tachy. We've slowed that down a bit at least.'

'QRS interval?'

'Ha, yes, you're right. That was our inclination too. It would be nice to know if she was taking tricyclics at a prescribed dose, or if she was completely naive to them.'

'Is that what you're going with then? Antidepressant overdose?'

'For now, it has to be.'

'No sign of her regaining consciousness yet?' Cathy asked, but Brodie snorted.

'Not a chance for now,' he said. 'If you do happen to hear any more about her home situation, can you let us know, Cathy? She'll have been moved upstairs by then, but call switchboard. Oh, and if you can get hold of any family …'

Cathy promised that she would try. She spent the rest of the afternoon attending to her patients having called through to Linda to thank her for covering earlier.

She had already called the police station. Unsurprisingly,

they weren't best pleased to hear from her so soon again. But what else could she do? She suggested that they nip down to the charity shop and take a look in the skip in case the girl who now lay unconscious, had found something. Cathy explained that someone from the shop had suddenly been taken seriously unwell but as yet she had no details. She supposed that the police would call the hospital and find out more themselves. Things had been decidedly quiet since Thomas had been run over and Cathy wondered in what direction their leads were taking them. Admittedly, it had only been a week since Betty had been killed, but so much had happened since then. Cathy thought of the young girl now lying on the renal ward. A possible tricyclic antidepressant overdose. The drugs were used less often nowadays for depression, but, occasionally, Cathy found them still being prescribed and had recommended them herself as a last resort. If only they knew more about this Holly girl, then things might make more sense. Cathy was sure that Holly was far more involved than they already knew. She had a sickening suspicion that if someone was going to overdose, they would hardly choose to do it when they were at work. It seemed likely, to her at least, that this stranger to the town, Holly, had been targeted. First Thomas Hogg, and now her. Both had known too much, and both had been silenced, although, Cathy hoped, not for long.

'James, have you got a minute?' she asked, tapping on his door and going in.

James looked up from his notes, his pen poised. 'Cathy, whatever's wrong? Come in and sit down.' He got up and ushered her to a seat, and then closed the door behind her. 'Well?' he asked, his eyes smiling. 'Was the afternoon that bad? I saw that you had to dash out? Anything serious?'

Cathy looked at her partner. He was so much older and wiser than she. He had seen so many people come and go and had cared for so many of them. 'James,' Cathy said. 'I'm not happy about Betty Scott's death.'

Her partner grimaced. 'Well,' he said half-laughing. 'Join the club, Cathy. No one in the town's happy about it. I assume you've heard the latest; that she was hit on the head before being left to die by the railway line? You're certainly not alone in being unhappy. And I also heard that Thomas Hogg is now in hospital, although I had assumed that the police were charging him.'

Cathy shook her head. 'No, oh no, James. It wasn't Thomas that killed her, although he may know more about it than he thinks he does. His mother was an inpatient up at Fernibanks. I saw it in the notes. I think that's why he was run over. The police released him without charge. I think he was targeted after that. It's commonly known that he was shouting and singing about knowing who the murderer was that night in the pub, although he was probably lying. He potentially knows something though, but what it is, I don't understand.'

'Cathy, you're talking in riddles,' James sighed.

'I know, I know,' she said sadly.

The pair of them sat for some moments in silence.

'James,' Cathy finally said, as if coming to her senses. 'Did you manage to get in touch with that old medical school friend for me?'

'Eric?' James asked. He leaned back in his chair. 'I did. I would have spoken with you earlier, but I've been concerned.'

'Oh?' Cathy asked. 'What about?'

'You,' he said seriously. 'You're burning yourself out again. Won't you let this all drop and leave it to the police?' Cathy's look must have spoken volumes because he sighed. 'I'll tell you then. It's not a pretty tale I'm afraid, but Eric did remember about it only too well. It was the end of the old psychiatric hospital. A good twenty years ago. A fire broke out in one of the buildings. It happened overnight, and no one was alerted until early the next day. By then, the building was simply a burnt-out shell. They found a body. One of Eric's colleagues had perished inside. He was a lead psychiatrist and well-respected. It came as a blow to the medical world. Thankfully, he was the only fatality and no patients died. As I say, it pretty much signalled the end of the place. It was run down before, of course, but following that, I suppose the health and safety folk started poking about and they found that the rest of it was about as bad. Poor electrics and cracks in the walls. You can imagine.'

'A tragedy, like you say,' Cathy thought aloud. She was still confused as to how the accident might fit in with Betty's death and the attempted murder of Thomas Hogg. 'I still don't see though,' she said. She looked at James. 'That's not all, is it?' she asked.

'Well,' James confessed, 'that was what everyone on the outside knew. Eric told me a good deal more.' He licked his bottom lip as if stalling for time before reluctantly continuing. 'The doctor, it seems, although well-thought-of in his younger years, had begun with some research project or other that hadn't been cleared by an ethics committee. He had been fixated on the idea that electric shock treatments might be of use to treat a whole host of ailments. You know, it's still very useful even now for select cases?'

Cathy nodded.

'Eric said that much of what this psychiatrist had been up to, only came out after his death. The man had kept meticulous notes, but his thinking was quite flawed. He used the shock treatment extensively on several patients; depression cases, anxiety, even on the learning-disabled. Naturally, it was covered up, especially when they found that he was experimenting with trying the treatment on non-sedated patients, something that would have been absurd.'

'Oh God, James, how horrible.'

James nodded. 'It had to be hushed up of course.'

'Well, I had expected something, but not that,' Cathy said. 'If one of those patients was still alive now, they might well feel a good deal of anger, not only towards the man who had done the experiments but perhaps the matron who could just have conceivably turned a blind eye to it.' Cathy thought of her recent visit to Thomas Hogg's poor mother, Flora. She recalled the woman's distress when she heard that Cathy was a doctor. 'Oh James, it makes me feel quite sick.'

'Stop thinking about it,' James advised, crossing his arms. 'The police will find out the person responsible. You'll only make yourself ill.'

Cathy grunted. 'You sound like my father.'

The older man smiled. 'I do rather see it that way sometimes.'

Cathy hesitated at the door. 'James? Did your friend say if the psychiatrist was married? Did he leave anyone behind? Children?'

James's brow wrinkled. 'I didn't ask about a wife or family. I assume not. Eric mentioned something about a couple of rather unsavoury allegations. Apparently, he wasn't the most respectful when it came to women.'

'Verbally or physically?'

James looked grave. 'Sexually,' he said.

Cathy was aghast. 'Oh, God. As if his experiments weren't bad enough!'

'Listen, this is all second- or third-hand though. All old gossip and none of it is relevant today. The man died in what sound like horrible circumstances. If he was inappropriate ...'

'With patients, James? Had he assaulted a patient?'

James sighed. 'This has to stop, Cathy. You're driving yourself mad.'

When Cathy left the room, she stood in the corridor for

some time thinking. Had Betty known about the dreadful psychiatrist? Had she seen what he was doing, experimenting on his patients? Even turning a blind eye would be enough to enrage his victims. In consulting her, Cathy wondered if the old woman had spoken out in fear, knowing that she was at risk. Had the original killer been reminded of the dreadful injustice all those years ago, and finding Betty still lording it up behind the till, had they then decided to take matters into their own hands once again? Had they set fire to the old psychiatric place, killing their tormentor all those years ago? Had they then decided that the business was still unfinished? Cathy felt even more determined after what she had learned from James. There was someone out there, intent on covering up their crimes, and it seemed that they would stop at nothing to do so.

## 29

Alex was waiting for her outside the shop. 'I should have met you at the house,' he said. 'Then, we could have gone together from there. I would have offered to drive but the car's in the garage.'

Cathy told him it didn't matter.

'It's an odd first date,' Alex said and caught her eye as if checking he hadn't overstepped the mark. 'Oh Hell, I've not signed out. Can you wait a second? Carol'll go nuts if I don't.'

He dived into the shop once more but was soon sitting in the passenger seat once again, grinning. 'Sorry. Think it's to do with fire regulations. They need to know how many people are in the place at one time. Are you really sure you want to do this? I mean, I'm sure you have your reasons.'

Cathy smiled. She checked over her shoulder that no traffic was coming, and pulled out into the road. 'I promise we'll talk more after. I know it seems strange, but I have to do this first. You've heard about your friend Holly, I assume?'

'She's gone up to the renal unit, they said to me. Wanted to know if I knew anything more about her, but of course, I don't know a thing,' Alex said.

Cathy smiled slightly as they drove, knowing that perhaps his plea of ignorance was too forceful. She had no claim on Alex though, and it was none of her business if he had been seeing this mysterious Holly. She wondered why he wanted to distance himself from her so greatly.

Cutting into her thoughts, Alex told her that it was the next left. 'I always look out for the tree,' he said. They drew level with a sycamore, and he said that they should park up and walk. 'It's that one there,' he said, pointing to the house. 'The last time I came was for his wife's birthday. He said he needed moral support. That was a year ago though. He'll get a bit of a surprise seeing us.'

They came in line with the hedge that bordered the garden. It had been trimmed and was quite sparse. The house itself was one of the more substantial properties in the area. Symmetrical and pleasing to the eye, and made of old, solid stone. As they walked up the path, a light came on by the front door. Cathy looked at Alex.

'I feel a bit funny all of a sudden,' she confessed.

'He's alright actually. He'll spin you a good story though, so get ready.'

He pressed the bell. From somewhere deep within the house it sounded, shrill and harsh. Cathy grimaced as she heard footsteps and then, against the now-lit hallway inside, she saw the man's figure approaching. The front door was ajar, leaving the porch open. The glass panel of the inner door distorted his uneven gait, making a grotesque caricature.

When Neil opened the door, he was indeed taken aback. 'Well, well, well,' he said, but almost immediately, he remembered himself and stepped sideways. 'You'd better come in then, hadn't you?'

'It's just a flying visit, Neil,' Alex said, standing aside to allow Cathy to go first. 'We don't want to disturb you.'

'A house call from the doctor?' Neil asked, smirking.

'In a way,' Cathy said as they were led through to the high-ceilinged living room.

Neil waved them to sit. 'All alone this evening too. Roslyn's gone out. Bingo,' he explained shaking his head. 'Nice to have a bit of peace.'

He offered them drinks, listing hot and cold beverages to no avail. Cathy would be glad to find out the information and go. She didn't take any great pleasure in prying into other people's business, especially when it was a sensitive subject such as this.

'So, Alex, what can I do for the pair of you? I certainly wasn't expecting this, and after all of the hullabaloo at the shop today too. I saw you arrived as one of our volunteers was being carted off, Doctor. I wondered if she was your patient. History of this sort of trouble, was there? Overdoses and the like? She was an unstable character, to say the least, but no doubt Alex has filled you in as he knew her so well.' The old man covered his mouth in mock horror. 'Sorry Alex, hope I've not put my foot in it.'

Cathy went to speak, but Alex answered for her. 'There was nothing I could tell Cathy in particular, and she wouldn't tell you if she was Holly's doctor anyway, Neil. Confidentiality, you should know that.'

The older man nodded and smiled. 'Of course, of course. Well, what can I do for you then, there must be a reason for this unexpected pleasure?'

'I wanted to ask for a bit of information, as it happens, Neil. It might seem like an awful cheek, but I don't think I'm breaching anyone's privacy in telling you that I had heard that you told a story which caused a bit of a stir in the charity shop not long before Betty died.'

Neil looked from Alex to her, clearly unsure what she meant. Cathy watched the man closely and saw the moment of realisation.

'You mean about the fire, I assume?' he asked.

Cathy nodded.

'Well,' Neil said leaning back in his armchair, clearly readying himself for a good yarn. 'I don't know that it has any bearing on the oddities that have been going on in Glainkirk recently.'

'I agree it seems unlikely,' Cathy admitted. 'Please humour me though. Alex has already told me in the car, but I wanted to hear it from you. Not so much the story, as how everyone reacted when you told it. Straight from the horse's mouth, so to speak.'

This tactic seemed to work wonders, and Cathy knew she had judged things correctly when the old man leaned forward and rubbed his hands together happily.

'It was a strange story,' he began, 'I don't mind telling you, it's kept me awake many a night, thinking of the poor chap who perished.' Neil got up. 'They all enjoyed hearing about it, I seem to recall. Although I was surprised that they didn't remember. When I came home and told Roslyn what we had been talking about that day, she reminded me of something I had quite forgotten.'

'Oh?' asked Cathy.

'Tricia. Well, she should have remembered because she was a student nurse up there. Roslyn said she didn't think she completed her training. They worked together for a short time, but she dropped out halfway through. I thought it odd that she hadn't said and she must surely have remembered. Perhaps she was just being quiet and not wanting to ruin my little bit of fun telling the tale,' the old man said. 'Anyway, if you wait a bit, I'll find the paper.' He shuffled to a bureau by the bay window. After raking in one of the drawers, he located what he was after. 'This was what I showed them all when I went back in after Christmas. Roslyn found it for me tucked away. Did Alex tell you about her funny turn? It's usually Carol who has those, isn't it?

Falling all over the shop, very unsteady on her feet. I've told Carol before, that she hares about the place far too fast.'

'Who?' Cathy asked. 'Who had a funny turn?'

'Betty,' the man said. 'Went all wobbly, and looked like she'd seen a ghost. Knocked her tea all over the place. Of course, she'd not been in there when we were talking about it before, had she Alex? I told my story in the kitchen and she was still out by the till. So, it was the first time in maybe a while since she'd been reminded.'

Cathy took the newspaper cutting and scanned through the report quickly. It didn't add anything to what she already knew. 'Did you know she was a matron up at the old hospital?' Cathy asked.

'Of course,' Neil said, receiving the paperback and returning it to the drawer. 'Used to see her regularly up there.'

'Oh?' It was Alex's turn to speak. 'How come, Neil?'

The old man turned slowly and grinned. 'Woodwork,' he explained. 'Didn't I say? I used to run a class with them. Only for six months or so, I did it. It was just before I bought the antique place on Broad Street. Kept me out of mischief, so Roslyn would say. Not my cup of tea and some sad cases up there.'

'Did you know the doctor who died, then?' Cathy asked, feeling that finally, they were getting somewhere.

'Don't recall his name,' Neil said, meditatively. 'Not much missed when he did die, by all accounts, despite the gruesomeness. Bit of a cad. The young girls didn't like working alongside him. Even Roslyn said that. Bit touchy-feely, and worse. Rumour had it that they locked their doors when he was on nightshift, prowling about the place. Don't think the patients liked him much either. That's what they said at the time anyway. Not missed a great deal. A bit like poor old Betty, I suppose,' he said, shrugging. 'Can't say anyone will miss her either, although, I know, no one at the charity shop would dare to admit it.'

When they were back in the car, Cathy looked out of the window. The sky was darkening now and the clouds were moving rapidly across the deep-blue.

'You've already put up with a lot from me,' she began, but Alex shook his head and laughed.

'Don't say that,' he said. 'It's been fine to spend any time with you, however strange. I honestly didn't expect to see you, and then when you randomly turned up in the shop, it was almost too good to be true. All these years I've wondered. I've thought of you often. And then, you actually agreed to see me. That, I didn't assume would happen either. You're this high-flying doctor now, and I'm, well, I'm an ex-cop doing odd jobs about the town.'

'What happened with that?' she asked. 'If you don't mind me asking. It's none of my business, really.'

He patted his leg. 'Retired after I bust my leg. Long story. A lot of hospital appointments and pain since it happened. I didn't want to leave if I'm honest. I was in a pretty dark place for a while. It wasn't long after Sally and I split, and it was a really difficult period in my life. I moved back up here to forget, but it wasn't that simple.'

Cathy nodded. 'I'm sorry.'

'I thought a lot about you after Sally and I, well, you know? I think we both sort of felt it back then, didn't we? Things were difficult though, and I was already ... Anyway, I'm not now, and I'm glad to see you. I'm in a better place too. I'm planning on starting a business of my own. I've been speaking to the bank about it this past month, and it's ready to go. Things have been looking up, and then you walk in. I'd hoped, well, maybe not even that. To pick up maybe, where things might have started back then. I assume you're not ...?'

'What? Married?' Cathy laughed.

'Well, not exactly Cathy, but you know, attached to anyone? I don't want any misunderstanding right from the word go.'

Cathy shook her head. 'No. I've been in no position really.'

'Career? You were always very smart.'

At this, Cathy snorted again.

'You were always smart at speaking to folk. That was something I noticed long ago. People liked to tell you things, just like now, when you worked your magic on Neil.'

'I suspect Neil would have told anyone his silly story,' Cathy said. 'He's a bit of a brag, isn't he?'

Alex nodded. 'So, what now? Did anything Neil say, actually help you? I assume you are wanting to get to the bottom of Betty's death, and that's what all of this is about? It's funny because it's exactly what Holly was trying to do too. I'll need to take better care of you though,' he laughed.

Cathy nodded but was thoughtful.

'Well?' he asked again.

Cathy turned to face him. They were sitting very close to one another, and his arm rested by the handbrake. She accidentally touched him as she turned.

'I was going to ask about Holly as it happens,' she said quickly. 'Please don't be abashed. I guess I noticed that there had been something between the two of you when I first came in the shop, and then the way Neil was carrying on …'

Alex was shaking his head. 'No. You've got that wrong,' he said. 'She came over to mine a couple of times, I'll admit that. We had a drink and that was about it. I asked about her home life, but she was so odd with me. So cagey about it all. I guess it put me off. Look, I'll not deny, I was rather flattered. She was a pretty girl. But troubled too. I felt sorry for her, in a way. That's all.'

Cathy grimaced. 'I'm not asking for myself,' she said, and

then laughed. 'Well, a bit, if I'm honest. But no, it's more this whole business, Alex. She knew something, and if we knew more about her, it might give us the answer. Quite apart from anything else, I'd like to know if she was on any medication or had a past medical history of any sort. It would help the hospital out. Her next of kin really should know she's unwell, that's if she has anyone.'

'So,' he said sighing, 'what are we doing now?'

Cathy wasn't sure what he'd think of her suggestion.

'Does breaking and entering sound like a hot first date?' she asked. 'I know it rather goes against your past occupation, but you'll know the tricks of the trade, I presume?'

## 30

He knew the address of course. At least he knew which block of flats, having walked up the road with her a couple of times in the past, so he said. On the two adjoining lots, both along Hopefield Avenue, was what looked like council housing. Low, slightly rundown bungalows of indistinguishable dimension and colour. Around the parking area, was a low privet hedge with a few small trees evidently planted recently.

Cathy parked the car not within the car park itself, but on the street. Several windows were lit in the flats, so Cathy hoped someone would allow them access to the building at the very least. As they got out of the car, she felt a sudden thrill of excitement. Would this be the evening when they found the answer to the mystery?

They approached the main entrance, crossing the road together and walking along parallel with the hedge. Cathy glanced up. A figure showed in one of the windows, lit from behind by the ceiling light. Cathy momentarily met the person's gaze.

'You never know,' Alex had said earlier in the car as they

drove. 'She might have hidden a key in case she lost hers. If she has, I guarantee I can find it.'

But Cathy felt less optimistic. She was determined to get into the flat that night though. They had to find out about the girl. At the very least, they must get a contact number for her relatives and let them know what had happened. She had rung the hospital once more before leaving work and had checked up on both her and Thomas Hogg. She was told that both of their conditions remained unchanged. Thomas was now recovering well, but the girl Holly was still unconscious. Cathy had wondered if gaining access to Holly's house might have been a police responsibility, but Alex had shaken his head. 'If the hospital hasn't alerted the police to the case, it's unlikely,' he had said. 'And presumably, if she's now stable, there's no real life-or-death hurry until she wakes.' Cathy knew that what he said was true, but she also felt that it was of vital importance that they find out what Holly knew, as soon as was practically possible. One person was dead, and two people had been injured already. The police didn't seem too concerned, but she certainly was.

The detective in charge of the case had left a message on Cathy's phone while they had been in visiting Neil, saying that nothing had been found in the skip behind the charity shop. Cathy was disappointed but unsurprised. Whoever had poisoned Holly, had of course gone out and removed whatever it was that was so incriminating. It was all so sinister and calculated. Cathy felt sure that Holly had known far too much.

The evening was growing darker, and the street lights had come on. Together, they crossed the car park, and coming to the entrance, Cathy climbed the stone steps first. She looked at the intercom to the left, and beside it; a list of flat numbers, eight in total, with names next to each. Holly's name wasn't on the list. She turned to Alex.

'It's only rented of course. She's hardly the kind of girl to slot in a little name tag when she moved to make it easier for the postie,' he hissed. 'Just press any and ask. Go on.'

Cathy, having done a thousand house calls to the area in the past, swallowed and pressed at random. She allowed her hand to drop and turned around to Alex who was nodding encouragingly.

There was a crackle and then a voice answered.

Cathy turned back and spoke into the intercom. 'Sorry to be a pest, I'm looking for Holly?'

'She's number six, not three,' the voice said angrily. 'I'm pissed off, folk pressing this buzzer like I'm some sort of domestic.' But the buzzer on the door sounded low and grating all the same, and Cathy quickly pushed.

'Thank you,' she said cheerfully to the intercom, but the angry recipient had gone.

'Six,' Cathy said as they walked into the lobby. There were three flats on the ground floor, and the staircase through another door on the left led them up to the next story. Cathy opened the door and checked that Alex was still behind her. Their feet echoed in the stone stairwell.

'Bit grim,' Cathy whispered.

'Yes, could do with better lighting,' he agreed.

They came to flat six and Alex immediately began snooping. First checking that her neighbours weren't looking, he stooped and lifted the front doormat outside.

'Anything?' she asked, but he straightened up empty-handed. 'Window ledges? Behind curtains? She might have left a key with one of the neighbours. Should I try?'

Alex was checking the landing outside the flat. He returned to the front door and looked in the letterbox, but snapped this shut without comment and then quietly, putting his shoulder to the door and turning the handle, he pushed. His face grimacing with the effort.

Cathy snorted. 'Don't be an idiot. I'll tap on four and five and see if they have a key or know how else we might get in.'

The occupants to the two flats were unhelpful, even when Cathy explained that she was a doctor and was concerned about the woman who might be inside the flat.

'Well, she's not inside,' the man in flat four said. 'She's gone, thank God. Keeps us up half the night playing her music and stomping about. I'd know if she'd come back. Vomited on the stairs the other week. Drunk half the time. God knows how the flat looks.' He had then unceremoniously shut the door in Cathy's face.

'Nice,' she said, stepping back. She turned again to her co-conspirator. 'Ideas?' she asked.

'Well, it was your scheme in the first place,' he said. 'Can't we just wait until she wakes up and then speak to her? This is all a bit over the top.'

'No,' Cathy hissed angrily. 'I thought you were going to be of use, but you're such a defeatist. I want this sorted tonight.'

'Well, I can't get you in this way,' Alex said.

She began to descend the stairs.

Alex followed. 'Are we heading home then?' he asked, but he should have known better. They exited the building and instead of crossing the car park, which was now quite dark, Cathy veered off around the edge of the block of flats, until she stopped by a metal cage that held all of the industrial-sized bins. She looked up at the window above. It was in darkness. She turned to Alex who stood despondently behind her, shaking his head.

'Come on, give me a leg up.'

As he half-carried, half-pushed her up onto the roof of the bin shelter, he cursed her a thousand times for her obstinate nature, but by the time she was up and grinning down at him breathlessly, wobbling and slipping on the icy surface, he was seemed over it and called out for her to be careful, for God's sake.

A quadrant of the moon was rising, but, for the moment, everything outside the reach of the street lamps was hidden in a dark shroud. Cathy clawed her way across the uneven roof, trying to be as quiet as she could. Behind her, she could hear Alex's repeated attempts to hoist himself up also, but she told him to wait until she was off the roof, fearing that it might not hold their combined weight. She came level with the window finally. Her fingers gripped the ledge, thankful for the extra security it gave her. The blind behind the glass of the window was drawn shut but there was a slot of the room visible at the base. Cathy looked up and saw an extractor fan, circular and grimy, inserted into the top righthand corner. It made sense that she had chosen the bathroom, but it must undoubtedly be the correct flat as the others on the floor were occupied and the windows lit. Cathy examined the window itself. It was new, which disappointed her. She had hoped that splintering and rotten, the bottom of it might easily be pried up. The handle, although not fully pulled down, had locked the window shut. Cathy attempted to jerk it open, but with little to hold onto, her fingertips slid and the window didn't move.

'Alex,' she called as loudly as she dared. 'I can't get it open. The handle's not totally down though.'

She could hear him tutting from below. 'If you'd let me get up there, I could have done it,' he hissed. 'You need something like a coat hanger.'

Cathy couldn't disguise her disgust at this suggestion. 'Well, I'm unlikely to have one of those to hand. Go and find me something. I'm fine waiting here, but don't be ages.'

She stood, becoming increasingly stiff with the cold, until after perhaps five minutes, she heard his footsteps jogging back around the edge of the building.

'Don't know if this will be any help,' he said, passing something up to her. 'It was tying up one of those newly planted trees at the front.'

Cathy removed one hand from the window ledge and slowly bent down and retrieved what he had placed on the roof.

'Right, listen,' he said. 'You need to slot it in the bottom of the window if you can. It may not be narrow enough and if it won't fit, I don't know what we'll try next. If you can thread it through a gap at the base, pull it along the underside of the window until it comes in line with the latch. Push as hard as you can. It might need a good bit of jiggling. With any luck, it'll pop open.'

Cathy smiled and without speaking, got to work. She wished that she had worn gloves because by now her hands were quite cold and painful. But spurred on by the task, she continued. The tree buckle was flexible and narrow. This meant that it was easy enough to insert into the gap in the window, but harder to manoeuvre along and gain any pressure on the lock. Cathy fidgeted with the thing, time and again withdrawing the strap and restarting the entire process. Below, she could hear Alex pacing back and forth, rubbing his hands to keep warm. He called up to her once and asked how it was going, but she was at a critical moment and didn't answer. When the window bolt finally popped, releasing the handle inside, Cathy nearly fell backwards in her excitement.

'Well done,' Alex called up to her, but now came the issue of getting inside.

'Alex, you'll never get through,' she whispered. Her heart was beating very fast.

Carefully, she grasped the bottom of the window and slowly raised it outwards. She ducked under it and gently pushed the blind aside. Cautiously, she leaned in and across the edge of the window. With infinite care, she edged forwards until she was, at last, lying stomach-down across the ledge. Her hips stuck in the gap and she had to wiggle herself free, finally resting her hands on either side of the toilet cistern that was conveniently below the window. Her ultimate move was ungainly and not without noise, but finally, she was in the bathroom. She stood still, listening, her heart hammering in her ears. She prayed that the neighbours hadn't heard and called the police. But no noise came to indicate that they had done so, and she leaned out again, calling down the Alex that she was OK.

As the flat was in darkness, and not wanting to turn on a light and draw attention to herself, Cathy switched on her mobile phone. She swung the screen display this way and that until she was familiar with her surroundings. The neighbour had been right in what he had assumed about Holly's lack of pride in her short-term home. The place was a tip. Cathy moved through to the main living area, seeing books and clothes strewn everywhere, but few personal belongings other than these. There were no photographs and no ornaments at all. On the kitchen table, Cathy found Holly's laptop, and beside it some papers and a notebook. She flicked through the pages, hoping to discover a name or address. She was shocked by what she read.

It looked as if the girl had been jotting down thoughts on the murder. On the first piece of paper, she had written: 'Numbers?' This had been underlined and she had gone on: 'Why so important? Speak to Thomas.' Cathy didn't understand where this line of inquiry was headed, so she moved on to the paper below. It appeared that Holly had been investigating each of the charity shop volunteers. Cathy read the line at the top of the page entitled: 'Connections with Fernibanks. Reasons to Kill.' Holly had documented Carol's name first, and beside it; the girl had written: 'Ex-social worker. Quit or dismissed? Why?' Below Carol, came Tricia. Holly had scrawled: 'Housewife? Possibly a psychiatric inpatient or nurse? How to access medical records? Would

Marie know?' Cathy didn't know who Marie was, but she thought it was a useful nugget of information at least. Then it came to Neil, and it seemed that the girl had not heard about his connection to Fernibanks, because all she wrote was: 'Idiot. Bigot. Antique dealer. Dodgy deals in shop.' Cathy smiled despite the seriousness of what she was doing, feeling that this said a lot about both Neil and Holly. She came of course to Alex, as she knew she must, and almost didn't want to read what it said. It seemed that the girl had done more research on him than on any of the others. Cathy straightened up, having read the words. She didn't know what to make of it all. 'Met. Police Division. PC dismissed. Gross misconduct. Unreasonable use of force.'

Cathy stood rooted to the spot and frantically considered something Alex had said earlier that evening. Why it hadn't occurred to her before, she didn't know. She suddenly remembered his excuse for not driving that night. His car was in the garage. Why was it in the garage? Was it because he had been in an accident the night before last? Was it Alex who, having killed Betty after she unearthed the truth about his dismissal from the police and threatened to expose him, ran over poor Thomas Hogg in an attempt to silence him also? He must have been keen to frame the vulnerable man, knowing only too well that police suspicion might fall on him if he strategically left a trace of blood outside his house. Only Alex would have had the ingenuity and criminal knowhow. Suddenly, it all became so obvious. Who else had known vulnerable, odd Holly well enough to spike her drink and poison her? It could only be one person. How foolish and trusting she, Cathy had been. She had been so desperate to renew his acquaintance too.

Just then, she heard a noise from the bathroom and turning, she saw Alex standing in the doorway. He looked across at her quizzically. Cathy's mouth went dry.

## 31

After what seemed like a lifetime of confusion and thirst, and not wanting to do so, because where she had been these last twenty-four hours was infinitely easier, Holly pulled herself back into consciousness. At first, her whole body ached in a quite sickening manner. She tried to unstick her tongue from the roof of her mouth, but it appeared to be lodged there for now. Exhausted, she gave up and drifted once more back to sleep.

When she next woke up, Holly tried opening her eyes. This she found, presented her with complete and debilitating sensory overload, and she hurriedly shut them and instead listened to the increasingly obvious beeping noises around her and the low hum of what she finally deciphered as voices. After a while, she decided to try the eyes again. This time, her left eyelid stuck, and for this small mercy, she was glad. Her right eye fluttered, and finally adjusting to the impossible brightness of the room, she began to see shapes. Slowly, Holly started to make sense of her surroundings. After some minutes, she concluded that she was in a hospital bed. This, she thought would do for now, and she again drifted into nothingness.

When Holly next surfaced, she did so more vigorously and although she was not perhaps aware, she called out.

'Better?' a nurse asked. 'You've been coming and going for a while now. You kept calling for your mother. If you can tell me her name and number, I'll try and call.'

Holly couldn't understand what she meant.

'Not to worry just now then,' the nurse said, frowning slightly. 'We've been rather concerned. You took something. I wonder if you even remember now?'

Holly clumsily said that she didn't.

'The doctors are doing their rounds soon and they'll explain what's been happening. You'll maybe want a sip of water to wet your lips. You've been getting fluids through a line since you came to us, but people always wake up thirsty.'

Holly didn't want to talk and lay motionless in her hospital bed watching as the nurses came and went. After a time, a group of doctors arrived and stood at the end of her bed and looked at her, but it was too much trouble to be interested in them. After asking her about a hundred questions, without receiving a reply, they left again.

Sometimes, during those initial hours of wakefulness, when Holly opened her eyes, she was aware of someone sitting beside her bed. At first, she thought it was part of a dream, and she grinned stupidly to herself and closed her eyes once more.

When she next woke up, the ward was in darkness. She looked for the figure beside her bed, but they weren't there anymore. Holly felt a growing sense of self-pity, but she swallowed this down, along with the medication a nurse brought her and fell asleep once more. The next day, much the same happened, but the visitor that she had wondered about was less of a hallucination and more of a reality. The person sometimes spoke to her. The voice was soothing and melodic. Holly knew that she was being read to, but didn't bother with the words.

The following day, having been troubled with vague thoughts all that night about a skip, Holly awoke feeling less tired and called for a nurse to ask who had been sitting with her on the previous day.

'Oh, I thought you were more aware of things. She said that she was family. A lady called Marie. Very patient with you. Lovely lady. She's been going between you and another man on the orthopaedics ward. Taking it turnabout to sit with you both and read.'

Holly nodded and smiled. Of course, it made sense.

At last, there came a time when she felt much more like herself and she was able to collect her thoughts and to put them into some sort of order. Her current situation was clearly at the forefront of her mind and several points needed to be addressed with some urgency.

The first was: what should she say when asked what she had taken to kill herself? She knew, from listening to the conversations around her, that this was exactly what the hospital staff had assumed. She had overheard one doctor asking a nurse if they had managed to get any more background information on her past psychiatric history and if she had been on the tablets for many years. She assumed, therefore, that they had yet to trace any of her family. This should have pleased her, but in some ways, she had wanted nothing more than to find that she had been outed and her family had come down to take her back home. Holly soon roused herself from this sentimental nonsense though. She had no home now after all, and the family that she thought was hers, never really had been. She decided, after much consideration, that if asked directly about the overdose, she would explain that it had been a moment of drunken madness. A friend had been on some tablets or other, and she had stolen them, not knowing what they were. She had taken them when she was intoxicated and feeling low. She had arrived at the shop the following morning, having forgotten what she had done, and it was only as the day had progressed that she had felt unwell. This seemed quite plausible to Holly, and she congratulated herself on her ingenuity.

The second point was harder, of course. Who was it that had tried to kill her? Holly felt sure that she had unearthed the only bit of physical evidence linking the killer to Betty's murder. She thought of the bag in the skip and the blood-soaked clothes that she knew would no longer be there. The killer would have long since re-disposed of these. It had been an audacious ploy to get rid of them in such a way in the first place. But now, what could be more daring than to poison her in broad daylight, in front of the other volunteers, having clicked that she had found the evidence? It was either an act of supreme boldness or one driven by sheer panic.

Holly thought back to that day in the cold when she stood knee-deep in binbags. She remembered the bathroom light at the back of the shop switching on and off, and a figure behind the mottled glass. They had seen what she was doing of course and had been forced to act quickly. Why, at the time, she hadn't considered her own safety, she didn't know. First Thomas, and now her. As she lay there alone save the beeping machines and the general hubbub of hospital sounds, she wondered how it had been done. How had they poisoned her? There had been a couple of opportunities, as she saw it. She wasn't sure what she had swallowed, or how long the stuff would have taken to work. She considered that day and what she had consumed. Before she began her hunt in the skip that day there had been a cup of tea. It had been a consoling mug after she had failed to find the imaginary ring. And then, of course, odious Neil had emerged halfway through her skip pillage and had tried to get her to drink another. This, she had refused at the time, but it did make her suspicious of the man's motives. She thought again of that freezing day. She considered it all. After making her discovery, she had gone inside. She had been confused and frightened, not knowing what to do next. She had sat in the bathroom trying to gather her thoughts.

It was only then, that Holly recalled who had tapped on the bathroom door, urging her to come out and warm herself up with the cup of coffee he had made. He had left it for her on the side table in the kitchen. There, for her to pick up. Of course. It made sense that it was him, and of all of the volunteers, it was he who she had most wished it not to be.

## 32

'You look like you've seen a ghost,' Alex said. He came towards her, his arms outstretched. 'What have you found?'

Cathy leapt back and knocked her hip on the kitchen table. 'Nothing,' she said, and then gathering herself, she laughed nervously. 'God, you made me jump. How on earth did you fit through the window? Give me a hand looking for any medication. You try the kitchen and bathroom. I'll look in her bedroom for an address book, although I doubt, we'll find anything.'

Alex moved away and Cathy, still shaking uncontrollably, but glad of the excuse to move, forced herself to go through the motions of searching the flat. All the while, the notebook with the words: 'unreasonable use of force,' was in her jacket pocket. Several times, she caught herself touching it in case it was visible, with the corner sticking out, but she knew she must not draw attention to it.

'Any luck?' he asked, joining her in Holly's bedroom. Cathy straightened up, having been looking on one of the bedside cabinets. The bedroom had revealed a good deal more about Holly. There were books and papers everywhere. Cathy had only glanced at a few, but seeing that they had no bearing on the case, she replaced them carefully, feeling guilty for having violated someone else's private domain. Alex approached. 'There's no medication anywhere. No prescription papers, nothing,' he said. 'I can't find an address either.' He was again too close. He moved even nearer towards her. 'I can't believe we're doing this,' he whispered, his lips twitching with a smile.

Cathy laughed and ducked past, avoiding his eye. 'Come on. We'd better get out before we're caught.'

He reached out to her and caught her sleeve as she passed. 'OK?' he asked.

She was afraid he was going to try to kiss her so she moved purposefully towards the door. 'We need to get out,' she repeated and pulled away.

They said little in the car as she drove him home. He must have known that it had all changed between them. But hopefully, he assumed it was because of her exhaustion and fear at what they had just done. More than anything, Cathy longed to get him out of the car. Now, every movement the man made, seemed sinister. Once, he accidentally touched her arm and she flinched as if she had been stung.

When she pulled up outside his house, there was a horrible awkwardness.

'Cathy?' he asked.

Despite her better judgement, she felt guilty, as if it were she who had let him down, instead of the other way about. 'Look I'm sorry,' she lied. 'I'm just overwrought and exhausted. I'm sorry I asked you to come on a wild goose chase this evening. It was a stupid idea and we could have ended up getting ourselves into trouble. I never meant for that to happen.'

He nodded, but she wasn't so sure he was convinced.

'We'll meet up properly,' she said. 'Go on a real date another time. Let's just wait until this is over with, OK? I feel like until this is done, I can't move on. I know I didn't know her personally, but she was my responsibility in a way; Betty, I mean. She came to me for help, and then she died, and horribly.' Cathy didn't even know why she said this. Perhaps to make him feel guilty. 'Anyway,' she said with finality. 'I need to get home. I want to go now.'

He got out of the car without saying a word. She turned the wheel smoothly and glancing in the rearview mirror, saw him standing in the street.

When she arrived home, she ran up the front path, and getting inside, she locked the door. Having done this, she moved around the house, checking that all of the windows were secure also. She didn't expect Alex to be so stupid as to come after her that night, but she felt she couldn't be too careful after all that had happened. Pouring herself a glass of wine, she cursed herself for having picked the most dangerous person to firstly, ask for help in solving the crime, and secondly, have feelings for. Ridiculous, she told herself angrily. Too fast and far too soon. They had only just met up again and then she found out this. She moved the notepad across the kitchen counter where she had left it. 'Unreasonable force'. What did that even mean? What had Alex done to be sacked from the police?

She thought of Holly's flat. So stupid. Such a risky position to put herself in. She thought of what she had seen there. Yes, the notebook, but there had been other things. Beside the computer, she had seen the folded paper. She had slipped it under the keyboard as Alex approached. But she had read the name. Was that why this girl Holly had come to Glainkirk? Had she found what she was looking for?

Cathy took a long swig of wine and began to relax. Thankfully her hands no longer shook. Her cat came through and settled beside her now in the living room where she had moved with Holly's notes. She had turned on all of the table lamps and had put on the electric fire too. Already, the place felt more secure and comfortable. Impulsively, she snatched up her mobile and scrolling down the list of numbers, she called Suzalinna. It had been ages since she last spoke with her and so much had happened since then.

'Well darling, you're right,' her friend said, 'a lot has happened. Two people in hospital now, you say? I wonder that the second one didn't come in on my shift. I heard about your heroics from Brodie, by the way. I was going to call. Actually, I did call and left a message, but you didn't get back to me. Too busy racing about the place, trying to unearth murderers. I must say, I was impressed when I heard about your minor surgery at the roadside. Treating a tension pneumo with a biro. Very clever darling. Very. You've achieved legend status with the medical students attached to the apartment anyway.'

'I thought you'd like that.' Cathy laughed. 'He's doing fine now. I rang the ward earlier and he's getting his chest drain out tomorrow.'

'And what about the other one, then?' Suzalinna asked. 'Poisoned, you think?'

'Yes. She was acidotic. Still unconscious. They think it was a tricyclic overdose, but I very much doubt she was prescribed them.'

'Well, it seems incredibly simple then, darling,' her friend said. 'Tomorrow morning you go into work and trawl the notes. If any of the people at the charity shop are on tricyclics, you have your murderer, and twice-over attempted murderer.'

Cathy didn't speak.

'Well?' Suzalinna asked. 'I'm right, aren't I?'

'It's more complicated,' Cathy confessed. 'I've found something out about one of them already. It's rather awkward now.'

'What another motive, you mean? That doesn't matter though, darling. From what you've told me, they all had a reason to kill really. No. Opportunity is what you need to look at now, and if you found out who actually had the drugs in their possession, it might lead you to the real killer. Focus on that.'

'Maybe,' Cathy said.

'Why are you dithering? Who is this person you've found out about?'

'You wouldn't believe it if I said.'

'Have you found out why the old woman went down to the railway anyway that night?' Suzalinna suddenly asked.

'You know, I went down there to look,' she admitted.

'And?'

'I felt a bit of an idiot doing it actually, but I think I saw where she crossed the fence and then, the path she took along the side of the line. There was blood still. I saw that. It was horrible.'

'Why did she do that though? Even if she was going to meet someone? I think you need to ask yourself the right questions, darling. What was an elderly woman doing grubbing about along the railway line? Listen, give me a shout if you need a sidekick. I think I'm pretty good at this detecting stuff. By the way, have you managed to track down Sally's gorgeous ex?'

Cathy laughed. 'I'll tell you about that another time,' she said, and much to Suzalinna's obvious indignation, she said good night.

Cathy found herself drinking another glass of wine. She was unwilling to go to bed, despite the obvious safety of her own house, and the comfort that Suzalinna's chatter had given her. Instead, she sat up long into the night, looking at the electric fire. It wasn't until her cat jumped on her knee and kneaded at her jumper, that she remembered the mark on the grass. The outline of a box of some sort. Not heavy though, but enough to flatten the grass.

'Clever,' Cathy said to herself. 'The perfect excuse to lure her there.'

But Cathy felt strongly still that she had neglected the original crime. Fernibanks did seem to be central in all of this. Was the doctor who perished lured to his death also, just as Betty had been? A perverted man, certainly in his scientific thinking but also, it seemed, in his relations with women. It seemed not impossible to imagine the dreadful man being induced to meet someone, a female, in one of the deserted buildings. Neil had proposed that the perpetrator had been Betty herself. The righteous matron. Had she known about the awful experiments on his patients? Had she asked him there, intending to kill him? Was that why she had been killed all these years later? Did someone want to avenge the man's death having had the incident brought up again by Neil and his insensitive anecdote?

Cathy thought of Betty. When she had come asking for help, she had assumed that she was the real victim. How differently things now looked though, if one considered Betty as a killer first. Was she afraid that with only limited remaining days, she might be outed? Had she come to Cathy for protection, hoping to swerve the retribution for her ancient crime? Cathy thought again of the blood she had seen on the grass verge and sighed. No one deserved that end, no matter what they had done. The old woman had been terminally ill already. Killed with a blow to the head first and then, to add insult to injury, she had been left lying in the path of a train. Cathy shivered. Why had the killer done that?

## 33

By morning, she was no longer afraid, but instead felt an aching sense of foreboding. Cathy decided that as far as relations with Alex went, there would be no more. How could she contemplate even communicating with a man she didn't trust? He had lied to her from the word go, and now, she could only hope that her investigation would not lead her back to his door. But despite the surprising sense of disappointment that this decision brought, she felt that she must not allow her better judgement to be clouded. Granted, Alex was definitely in the frame, but she really must look into the other volunteers also, just as Suzalinna had suggested.

The afternoon had been allotted to booked-in patients and paperwork. It was true that she had neglected the practice a good deal these past few weeks, but despite this, she felt that she must put her admin time to use and continue the investigation.

It was unfortunate that she didn't know the surnames of the two ladies in question. Tricia and Carol were very ordinary names after all, and within their age-bracket also, they were hardly unusual. Cathy walked through to the front desk.

'Have you got a minute, Michelle? I'm trying to do a bit of

fundraising for the charity shop tombola in a couple of weeks. Can we put a couple of these things up? Carol, one of the volunteers gave me it.' Cathy held up a poster. 'I'll be collecting prizes for the thing too. Goodness knows how I got roped in.'

Michelle giggled. 'We'll put it up on the notice board Dr Moreland if you leave it there.'

'They're a funny bunch of women,' Cathy said. 'Are any of them ours, do you know? I thought I recognised a face perhaps.'

'Patricia Bonnar? Is that maybe who you mean? She's been on our list for years. Sees Dr Longmuir, I think. Bit of a frumpy, old sourpuss. Well, that's my impression. Typical charity shop material though. Do-gooder but needy, if you get me? I can't remember what she comes into Dr Longmuir for. You'd need to ask him, or look her up.'

Cathy nodded. 'Do you know about the other one? I think she's called Carol. She's the one in charge and who all my dealings have been with.'

Michelle shook her head. 'I don't know her, no. Perhaps Dr Longmuir might? They do get a regular turnover of staff, I think. I walked past the other week and saw a new one rearranging something in the window.'

Cathy thanked her. As she passed James's room returning to her own, she heard his voice speaking reassuringly. She'd wait until he had finished with his patient and then ask. Sitting down, she typed in the name: 'Patricia Bonnar.' There was only one match. With a couple of clicks of the mouse, Cathy was looking at the fifty-six-year-old woman's notes. It seemed that the lady was a regular, consulting James every two months or so. Cathy looked at her past prescriptions and was relieved to find that, although the woman was on an antidepressant, it was not a tricyclic. James had prescribed one of the newer kinds, which would certainly not have caused any serious ill-effects at a high dose, such as the one that had poisoned the girl Holly. It seemed, then, that Tricia was out of the frame for now. That of course, left Carol, who Cathy still couldn't pin down with a surname. Cathy waited a frustrating fifteen minutes until at last James's door was opened and she heard him saying goodbye to his patient. Before her partner had a chance to call in the next, Cathy nipped into his room.

'James,' she said.

Her senior partner looked up in surprise. 'What are you up to Cathy?' he asked.

'I need information,' she said bluntly. 'The charity shop ...'

At this, James rolled his eyes.

'No, give me a chance, James,' she pleaded. 'I've just been looking at Patricia Bonnar's notes ...'

'Cathy,' he said, warningly. 'You're on shaky ground. You know all accesses to notes are logged and auditable. Code of conduct? It's unethical to be raking through the files unless it's for a medical purpose.'

Cathy shook her head in annoyance. 'James, are you for real? Honestly, I am doing it for medical reasons, I'm protecting the community. If you hadn't noticed, a patient of ours was murdered the other week, and another two people have been hospitalised since. Something very nasty is happening in Glainkirk and I'm struggling to sleep easy knowing that we might be sitting next to a murderer day-in-day-out.'

'It makes me very uncomfortable, Cathy, you looking through the notes, that's all I'm saying. I agree that you needed to look at Thomas Hogg's because the police were due to come in anyway, but anything else is overstepping the mark. We pledged to uphold the code –'

Cathy raised a hand. 'Alright James, have it your way. I'll not look at anything. I'll not ask you about it either.'

She left the room and returned to her own, furious at James, but more so at herself for having been so thoughtless. He was of course, quite right. Since Betty's death, she had made a number of poor decisions. She wondered what James would say if he knew about last night's escapades, breaking and entering into someone's flat. Cathy brooded on it for some time, but eventually, she snatched up the phone. The call was short but she gained the information that she needed. She was about to put a call through to the hospital to enquire about the condition of Thomas Hogg and Holly, but impulsively, she replaced the phone and instead marched to the front desk.

'I'm heading out,' she told Michelle and jogged from the building into the rain.

∼

'WE'VE NEEDED to talk for some time,' she said. 'I've been biding my time and waiting. I knew that the answer must lie with you.'

Holly, pale and thin, stared back at her blankly. Her hair lay lank across the pillow in a knotted cascade. Her fringe fell over her eyes and the girl, too weak to raise a hand, blew at it with the corner of her mouth. The rest of the hospital ward continued around the two women, but Cathy was oblivious.

'I didn't know how long you'd take to wake up,' she confessed. 'Last night, I'm ashamed to admit, I was in your flat.' There was a flash of interest from the girl's eyes and Cathy shrugged and laughed. 'Hardly the kind of behaviour you'd expect from a GP, but then I suppose we're not that dissimilar, are we Holly?'

The younger woman stared back at her but didn't speak.

'I saw the textbooks. The notes.'

It was the first time the girl spoke and her voice was low. 'I've quit.'

Cathy smiled at this and shook her head. 'Perhaps,' she said. She had seen the pages of revision by the girl's bedside table. If she was done with her medical degree, then she had a funny way of showing it.

'How about I speak and you can jump in and correct me?' When the girl didn't answer, she took it as her assent. 'You came to Glainkirk for a reason, that's clear. I knew that you were smart as soon as I set eyes on you, but troubled by something, that was obvious.' The girl sneered but Cathy continued. 'I think you joined the charity shop, as much to keep yourself busy as anything else. You've been working all through your school days and then at university. I doubt that you'd find it easy to suddenly stop and do nothing. I don't know if you saw the shop as a route to the answers you so desperately wanted. Perhaps, it just turned out to be that way. I called a colleague of mine up at the medical school in Aberdeen. You left after failing your anatomy exam. You hadn't told them about the extenuating circumstances for failing though. I believe your mother was eventually contacted by the deanery when you didn't show for the re-sit.'

'She's not my mother.'

'Yes. I heard about that too. Your family have been concerned. The medical school have worried also.'

The girl's cheeks reddened. She stared angrily at Cathy.

'I'm sorry,' she said. 'Your father, or the man who brought you up as his own, died only a few months ago. Your family hadn't told you before, and I suppose that during the trauma of his unexpected death, a heart attack, I believe, you discovered something that you were never meant to know.' Cathy paused and looked at the girl, who if anything, seemed to grow smaller and more fragile.

'Papers,' Holly said in almost a whisper. 'Then I forced my mother to speak.'

'You found out that you were adopted, didn't you? I'm sorry. I saw the birth certificate. It was lying beside your computer. Not much to go on. A common-enough first name for your birth mother, and a place: Fernibanks, Glainkirk. Neither your adoptive mother nor father had ever suggested that it might be the case. You had been an unusually clever child, out-performing the entire family, so I hear. The first to go to university, I believe. Certainly, the first to study medicine. Perhaps you never felt you fitted in? Medical school was meant to be where you blossomed, but then your adoptive father died and it was all too much.'

'They hate me. I'm not like them,' the girl said, and Cathy might have laughed if the situation had not been so serious, for the girl sounded so young.

'No, they don't hate you at all. Your family are incredibly proud, but you are different. You don't think like them. You are a very intelligent person, from what I hear. The university sees great potential in you. You can be a bit fierce and volatile at times. The alcohol hasn't helped, I suppose.'

A smile flickered on the girl's lips. 'That's the only good thing about being unconscious. I've done cold turkey without even noticing it.'

'You saw from the papers, that your birth mother was from Glainkirk. That's why you came, am I right?' Cathy continued.

Holly nodded. 'Yes. I didn't have much to go on, other than where I was left and the name.'

Cathy leaned back in her chair. 'Fernibanks and Elizabeth. Yes, I can see why you made the jump. The name, the place and, of course, the date seemed right too. I don't suppose you ever asked Betty?'

The girl shook her head. 'She wasn't really that sort of a person. She wouldn't have hugged me and told me she was sorry. I was going to speak to her though. I'd made up my mind to do it.'

'But then, she was murdered.'

'Oh, you know as well as I do that it was Alex,' the girl said angrily. 'He used to be a policeman. He was sacked for misconduct. I found that out looking it up and matching the dates. He was the one who poisoned me too. He knew how to frame Thomas, and when he was shouting that he'd seen who had killed Betty, he ran him over.'

'His car's being fixed in the garage,' Cathy said distractedly.

'There you go,' Holly said. 'He's the one. I suppose Betty found out the truth about him too and didn't like him working in the shop or something. The nurses told me I was poisoned with a tricyclic antidepressant. I did do some reading at medical school and I know that they aren't just used for low mood.'

'Neuropathic pain,' Cathy said.

'Exactly. I know you fancy him, and all that. I'm very happy for you but ... Who's the only person with a gammy leg, after all? It has to be Alex.'

Cathy nodded sadly.

'What did you mean about numbers, by the way?' Cathy suddenly asked. She had forgotten all about the first piece of paper she had found in Holly's flat.

Holly screwed up her nose. 'Stupid idea really. Thomas has an obsession with numbers and times. It's been going on for years according to Marie. I just thought it odd and wondered where it started. The night before he was run over, he arrived at my door saying he thought he was going to die, that he'd seen a number, and that everyone had a warning or a time when they were going to die.'

The girl looked utterly exhausted and they sat for some time in silence before Cathy left her to sleep. There was only one thing for it. She felt she really must check there and then.

It took around twenty minutes to get to the bottom of things. Having left the orthopaedics ward, Cathy was still unsure how the new piece of information might fit. Thomas had been reluctant to share with her his prize possession. After all, he told her he had kept it near enough twenty years, carried it for safety in his bag everywhere he went. Cathy promised she'd take great care of it. One thing was for sure anyway, she needed to clear up a suspicion. It had to be done, whether she liked it or not.

Sally, her old friend from medical school, answered on the third ring. She was delighted, if a little surprised, to hear from her so rapidly after the reunion. Cathy wished she had called her far sooner though. It might have put an end to all of this a long time ago.

'Oh no, Cathy. I'm delighted to hear from you, but you've got your facts quite wrong. Oh dear, what a muddle, but how nice you've met up with each other. Alex did retire legitimately. It was during a car chase that he was injured. The other officer who he was with at the time though, went a bit overboard. I think he was too rough with the person they arrested. Alex was caught up in the whole thing. I think he had to testify against his colleague. We were barely functioning as a couple at that point, and it was the final nail in the coffin. He was depressed and drinking too much when he had to stop work. He had a family history of depression. His mother I think was quite bad. I'm glad he's moved on though, and back to Glainkirk too, how funny. Send him my love if you see him again. I'm so glad I went to that reunion, Cathy. To meet up with you again, and Suzalinna.'

Cathy agreed that they must keep in touch. When she hung up, something that Sally had said, struck a chord. She quickly called the practice and asked if James was free.

When she spoke to him, he was a little annoyed at her request, but he did agree if it would put an end to all of this nonsense.

'You're making yourself sick, I've warned you,' he said before hanging up. 'You've got a duty to your patients to stay healthy. Doctors can't be unwell. It affects too many people.'

## 34

Three days later, and a Saturday, Shirley's, the dreadful café on the Glainkirk high street, was thankfully quiet. The girls, who had served Thomas and Holly the week or so before, had reserved the largest table by the half-frosted, glass window at the front. Holly had already positioned herself next to a heater on the wall, and from there, she was able to watch the customers coming and going. She still wasn't quite her normal self and had lost a good deal of weight since her hospital admission, but with follow-ups to check her kidney function, she had been told she was going to be fine.

It didn't surprise her in the least to see Thomas's arch-enemy Carbolic, sitting at a small circular table in the far corner of the café. The man looked sulky and shambolic. It seemed strange that he had a habit of turning up where he wasn't wanted, or supposed to be. But Holly guessed that this completed the group in a way, with only Thomas, the single absentee from proceedings.

Carol and Tricia pitched up first. Like a pair of silly schoolgirls, they entered the café, giggling, carrying on, fussing over removing their many layers. Placing their felted jackets over the backs of the chairs, they then repeatedly dropped gloves, scarves, hats and whatever else they carried, under the table.

Holly thought that they were all a little uncertain of one another in these most unusual circumstances. Being outwith their normal environment of the shop did feel rather strange. Carol raised a hand in greeting to Carbolic who must have been watching in incredulity as more and more members of the charity shop staff arrived. Not long after, Alex and Neil walked in.

Holly wasn't sure if one of them had driven to the place. Perhaps Alex's car had been fixed by now. At any rate, when they arrived, the men were less wrapped up than the ladies. This did not go unnoticed and there was much jocularity from Neil about the weaker sex. Fortunately, it seemed that Holly was left entirely out of this crass generalisation. It was just as well because she was in the frame of mind to shoot Neil down pretty quickly if he started up any of his drivel. He did, however, give her a wink, and say that it was nice to see her up and about again. As it happened, they all acted as if Holly's stay in hospital had been an embarrassing mistake; something that no one dared address.

Alex looked away when he saw her, which indicated to Holly that he had indeed been fooling around with that Cathy doctor-woman. Holly didn't much care either way. Alex was far too old for her anyhow, and she had only been messing about.

In the beginning, there was the general chit-chat that one might expect, but having suggested the impromptu meeting herself, Holly felt that she should start things off. She waited for Neil to finish with his inane jabber; an elaborate story about his wife's car being involved in a minor collision due to the ice, or some such rubbish. Holly could tell that no one else was interested, and towards the end of the narrative, the others were beginning to glance around them. Even Alex looked at her in an odd way, making Holly feel quite sick. Finding a lull in the conversation, she cleared her throat.

'Thanks for coming everyone,' she began, and Carol looked at her suspiciously, probably for having the nerve to speak up, but also perhaps, for having been able to do so in such a civil manner. 'It was my idea to meet,' Holly went on.

The waitress had, by this time, brought teas and coffees. Unable to shake her unconventionality, Holly had ordered a hot chocolate and was horrified to find out exactly what this consisted of. The waitress presented the monstrous goblet as if Holly had won some kind of a prize, stepping back from the table with a flourish. Holly caught Alex's eye and he was smirking, knowing full-well, she assumed, that she would be unable to ingest the bloody thing without some degree of discomfort or mess.

'I suggested we meet,' Holly went on, ignoring the drink for the time being, 'as we hadn't managed the Christmas get-together, what with the business over Betty and then obviously my little misfortune.'

Carol nodded. 'No one was in a fit state for it really,' she said. 'But hopefully, things will return to normal. The police called me this morning. I've told Tricia already, but I've not yet had a chance to say to everyone else, and I knew we'd be meeting up anyway.'

'So, what's the story?' Neil asked, replacing his oversized teacup in its saucer, and spilling the liquid over the side. It seemed that the man was incapable of drinking a cup of tea without disgracing himself.

'Well,' Carol began, 'They said that the funeral is permitted to go ahead now. I've already done a bit of research myself.' At this, Carol looked a trifle embarrassed. 'It seems that having no family, and no savings to speak of, we might be required to club together a little. Just as part of the charity. That would give her a quiet sendoff.'

'What, us personally?' Holly couldn't help asking.

Carol turned to her somewhat annoyed. 'For those of us who are in a position to afford it and are willing to do so, then yes. For the others, I wouldn't dream of expecting it. The charity bosses themselves may well want to contribute anyway.'

'Well I guess ...' Neil began, but it was becoming farcical and Holly interrupted.

'I don't suppose the police mentioned to you, Carol, about the identity of Betty's killer, did they?'

Carol met her gaze steadily as if challenging her for speaking out of turn.

'Well Holly, it's interesting you say that. They never did find any of the bloodstained clothing,' Carol said accusingly, 'that you, apparently said you found in the bottom of our skip. There was no evidence of wrongdoing at all.'

The other volunteers looked shocked.

'Why did you say that?' Tricia asked, but Holly didn't answer. She was too busy glaring at Carol.

'So, I take it, they're no further forward then? The police, I mean,' Neil said. 'Still of the thinking that it was Thomas, or some stranger, or whatever?'

Carol smiled. 'That's not quite what they said, but I suppose so.'

There was silence. Holly's heart was beating so loudly in her ears that it nearly deafened her. 'But we know that's untrue, don't we?' she said and looked around at the group of volunteers. 'What about Thomas?'

There was a murmur of acknowledgement, but it seemed that Tricia was confused.

'You mean crazy Thomas who comes into the shop?'

'Yes Tricia, that's who I mean,' Holly said. 'Mad, crazy

Thomas. The local joke. The comical buffoon that we all like to take a pop at for all of his absurdities. He had an accident the other night, as you all heard. Everyone assumed that he had drunkenly walked in front of a car, but in reality, it was rather different. Run over and left for dead. He's currently recovering from what might have been life-threatening injuries, had it not been for the quick-thinking of Dr Moreland, our local GP-friend. Unfortunately, for the attempted murderer, despite being half-cut and as unreliable as the buses around here, Thomas didn't die, and neither did I, when I was deliberately poisoned.'

There was a gasp from Tricia. She covered her mouth, and her eyes were wide and alarmed.

'Bit of a surprise, Tricia?' Holly asked cruelly. 'But surely not. I'm hardly the type to take an overdose.'

The woman looked desperately at Carol, who returned her stare, stony-faced.

'Surely, it can't come as such a shock to you,' Holly went on. 'Apparently, it was a strong antidepressant. Admittedly, sometimes it's prescribed for nerve-type pain. Anyway,' Holly said, turning her gaze back to the rest of them. 'It puts a different perspective on things certainly. Had it been as simple as a single murder, I suspect that it might have been more easily brushed under the carpet, but given that the person has attempted to kill again twice-over, the police won't just let things go stale, of that I'm quite sure. Isn't that right, Alex?'

Alex, who had been scrutinising his hands, looked up suddenly as if he'd been darted.

'I don't want to out you, Alex,' Holly said, 'but you do have rather a different take on things than the rest of us, having been in the force yourself. Perhaps you'd like to tell us why you retired. Gammy leg, wasn't it? Did you need very strong painkillers for that?'

Alex shook his head, but wouldn't look at her. 'I thought you were different,' he said quietly.

'No, I'm not when it comes to murder, Alex.'

Neil put a hand on the other man's arm.

'Alright mate,' Neil said. 'We don't think it was you.'

'That is understanding of you, Neil,' Holly said, turning to the other man. 'You find yourself able to empathise, perhaps because you had a few secrets of your own also. I think everyone in the shop is all too aware of your shady dealings. Snaffling off stock for a low price and selling it on privately for your own ends. I suggest that you, more than anyone, should put your hand deep in your pocket and fork out something towards Betty's funeral.'

They all looked at Holly as if she was quite mad. Even Carbolic, who had been thus far unobtrusive, had managed to inch his way to the table beside them and was clearly listening in. The waitress came across at that point and they all pretended to be normal. She wiped a spill on the table and removed some cups. No one said a word.

When they were alone once more, Carol spoke. Her voice was bitter. 'You know everyone's secrets,' she said, maliciously. 'It might surprise you to know that Tricia and I did a little digging of our own and found out why you're not in work yourself currently. You made a few slips up in conversation that gave it away. I know you liked to play down the niceties, but the overinflated ego and intellect did seem rather out of place in a charity shop.'

It was now Holly's turn to look at the ground, but hating herself for doing so, she finally met Carol's stare unblinkingly, knowing that her own face must be ashen.

'Drunk and disorderly,' Carol said. 'And training to be a doctor as well. Utterly abhorrent. I assume you have some mental health problem and that's why you are the way you are. You never fitted in here anyway. Perhaps you should return to your medical school up north. That's if they'd even have you back.'

'Oh, they will without a doubt. I've already checked,' she said, and the volunteers all turned to look at Dr Cathy Moreland, who had just come in the shop. She stood in the doorway, stamping her feet on the mat and smiling. 'Sorry I'm late, Holly,' she said. 'I've just been making a few phone calls. I hope I've not missed too much.'

## 35

'Well,' Tricia said. 'I didn't sign up for this kind of discussion at all. I think we should call time on this supposed get-together.'

Cathy thought it a rather brave statement. But of all of the volunteers, Tricia was the one she knew least about. She watched in silence as Tricia began to collect her things.

'I'm sorry. We're not quite finished yet,' she said quietly.

Everything seemed to go completely still. Cathy's breathing was the only thing she was aware of for that moment. She ran her tongue over her lips.

'Well, I don't want to hear any more of this,' Carol said, beginning to push her chair back also and to get her coat which was hung on the back.

When finally, Cathy spoke, it felt as if she had been silenced for too long, and the words almost fell from her mouth. She had been so foolish.

'I took too long,' she said ruefully. 'For that, I am very sorry. Please sit-down Carol, Tricia. We must get to the truth. Glainkirk has suffered quite enough already.'

The two women tutted but took their seats once more.

'I suppose my story starts some twenty years ago. Neil set the whole dreadful thing in motion that day when he spoke about the old psychiatric hospital. It brought back a lot of unwanted memories. Almost all of you had a connection with Fernibanks, as it happens. Some, a deeper connection than others. Neil, you, for example, were a woodwork tutor up there for a short time. Not a huge role, but of course, you too, were first on the scene following the dreadful tragedy.'

Cathy looked around the faces of her listeners, trying to judge how next she should go on.

'I must admit that I had a bit of luck finding out about the man who died in the fire. We were all quite aware that he was a disreputable psychiatrist. I think there was a suggestion that he might have been behaving in a highly inappropriate way. Not many knew the extent of his corruption though.'

'What did he do?' Alex asked.

Cathy turned and smiled. 'I found out from my senior partner. It seems that the psychiatrist had been experimenting with the use of electric shock treatment. I think that the other doctors were extremely uncomfortable about it, especially when they found out that he was trying the treatment out on non-sedated patients, something that would have been utterly appalling to experience, and even more so in a vulnerable state.'

Alex shook his head. 'Horrible. How could anyone?'

Cathy looked seriously at him. 'Someone at the hospital was just as disgusted. The doctor, it seems, didn't die accidentally in the fire. His remains were found. It was difficult to be clear, but it did seem that he had sustained a head injury, and not only that, he had electrodes on his temples.' Cathy looked at Alex, afraid to see anyone else's reactions. 'He was killed twice-over. Electrocuted and burned.'

There was a stunned silence.

'A bit like Betty's death, in some ways,' Cathy went on. 'I

always thought that it was far too excessive. It indicated anger of such force, that it was almost bordering on insanity. Hit over the head and then thrown in front of a train. I have struggled to connect all of you to the hospital, although I felt sure you must be. Neil, I have already mentioned. Alex, you too were a puzzle, until I learned about your family history of depression. Your mother was an inpatient for a short time, I believe?'

Alex nodded. 'She killed herself while she was there,' he said mechanically.

Holly gasped and looked as if she was going to speak, but Cathy continued: 'Carol, you were a social worker for a spell and presumably you had dealings with the place through your work. Tricia, I hear you were a trainee nurse. I suppose that you all might have seen what was going on up in that hospital and decided to take things into your own hands.' Cathy took a deep breath but no one spoke. 'But coming back to the present day, and Betty's visit to my surgery. I offered the poor woman a deadly diagnosis. Betty only had months to live. She spoke to me about being concerned about something in the charity shop. I wondered if she had, up until then, been keeping an eye on someone. She had realised that they had killed the psychiatrist, but had kept quiet about it all of these years. I think that she had had a conversation in the charity shop with that person recently. She told them that she was dying and couldn't leave this world without speaking out. She tried to convince them that they should own up. Betty was mildly religious, perhaps she couldn't conceive of the truth dying with her, even if she sympathised with the killer's reason for committing the crime. Betty was quite moralistic. She even gave me a dressing down when she thought I was putting my patients at risk by not spreading salt on the icy car park outside. Anyway, when she spoke to the killer, she sealed her own fate.'

Cathy looked around at all of the volunteers.

'Poor Betty was lured to the railway line. It took me a while to work out how. All it took was knowledge of her beloved pet cat. The murderer had simply to tell the old lady that they had seen her cat down by the tracks and Betty would have been beside herself with worry. Betty, along with her cat basket, the imprint of which I discovered on the grass by the railway, went down that evening after work. She perhaps wasn't aware of how much danger she was in when she saw her assailant. I certainly hope not. It must have been over very fast. After killing her, the murderer then returned to the shop, the closest place to change. They removed their bloodied clothes, and cleverly left them outside the shop in a binbag, to be disposed of the next morning. It rained that night, and I hear from Holly that the floor was bleached the following day. She also told me that a cat basket had been handed into the shop, also left by the murderer. She came across it in the skip when she was hunting for evidence, but of course, thought nothing of it. There must have been a good bit of tidying up to do, and then there was the quick trip down to the sheltered housing complex where Thomas lived, to leave a little incriminating evidence to throw the police off the scent. I don't think Thomas was a target in particular. It might have been anyone living up there.'

'Horrible,' Holly said. 'And then Thomas was shouting and stomping around, telling people he knew who the killer was, and me, well, I found the evidence. I had to be shut up too.'

'Thomas knew a good deal more than any of us realised,' Cathy said. 'Remember his obsession with numbers and times, Holly? I found out where that started. It was when he was a boy. I know Neil, you discovered the psychiatrist's body in the burnt-out building, but someone had been there before. Too young and confused by what he had discovered, and perhaps not even realising at the time that the man was dead, young Thomas Hogg rooted in the psychiatrist's pockets. I think, if truth be told, he was hoping to find some money, but instead, he found this.' Cathy reached in her pocket and withdrew a torn scrap of paper. On it was written: 'Eight o'clock.' Thomas kept his treasure all these years. He assumed after finding it, that everyone received a time, just before they were about to die. He was always on the lookout for his number.'

The room was silent. Cathy took a deep breath and continued.

'The psychiatrist had been given a time to meet in the deserted building. I can only assume that he thought it was for romantic reasons, but his assailant had other ideas. He was killed in cold blood. Betty must have seen the assailant fleeing the building. She kept it quiet all these years. She probably had greater reason than most for wanting the man dead anyway but the murderer wasn't ready to hand themselves in for anyone.'

The room was quite still.

'So, the police know?' asked Holly.

'Oh yes. It couldn't go on any longer,' Cathy said. 'You brought the notebook?'

From under the table, Holly produced the A4 diary that had been on the charity shop counter. Inside was written all the volunteers' initials and the times they were starting and finishing. 'The writing is faded and a little burned,' Cathy said, looking at Thomas's scrap of paper. 'It's just possible that a handwriting expert might be able to make a match. I admit it's a longshot ...'

The volunteers remained frozen.

'And the only other evidence that I found in the skip has now gone,' Holly began. 'What about the tablets I was poisoned with? I thought you said that might lead you to who it was?'

Cathy smiled. 'Maybe as a trainee doctor, you can tell us the side effects of tricyclic antidepressant medication, Holly.'

The girl smiled and nodded. 'Postural hypotension, tachycardia and dry mouth. In other words, dizziness on standing ...'

But she didn't need to go on. All eyes turned as the chair screamed on the linoleum flooring. Carol's face was like a mask.

The bell on the door sounded with another customer entering the café, but no one looked to see who it was. The table was mesmerised.

'I think,' Cathy went on, 'that the social work thing confused me. I assumed of course, that you had been up at the hospital in a professional capacity. I, of all people, should have known that just because you were working, didn't mean you were mentally well.'

When she spoke, her voice was odd and cracked. 'You've no idea what I suffered. None of you.' Tricia reached out a hand but Carol recoiled. 'Don't touch me. I don't want your sympathy.' Her face was almost grey, her lips, a dreadful mauve. 'I went into that place with a nervous breakdown. They were meant to help. Instead, I came out irreparable. That man. What he did to us with his 'new, experimental treatments' ...' She looked at Cathy with contempt. 'You think you understand? You don't know anything. None of you. Imagine being strapped to a bed, all the while, knowing what was coming. I willed myself to die so it would be over.' She looked around the group, taking each of them in, her eyes narrowed, full of pain and fury. 'And then, as if that hadn't been bad enough, how do you think it was for me? I finished one torment and began another. All these years living in fear. That bitch, Betty! She'd seen me. Said she spotted me running from the building. Her office looked out onto it, of course. She told me it was our secret, that she understood why I'd done it. I thought I was safe. But gradually, I began to realise what she meant. I was never free after that. They might as well have locked me away. She watched over me all these years. Just a raised eyebrow. Just a little remark. That was enough to let me know that she still had power over me. It was torture. Far worse than what that doctor ever did. And then,' Carol's voice climbed. 'And then, she had the cheek to tell me it was time to confess! Time to own up to what I had done. All to appease her conscience when she was dying. She said it to me as if she had done me a favour all these years. Said that I'd had a good life and the police wouldn't be harsh when they heard why.'

Cathy turned to the door. Carol had failed to notice that the last customer entering the café, had been the detective inspector who had interviewed them originally in the shop.

∾

CATHY AND HOLLY stood in the cold, on the pavement outside, watching the police car wend its way up the high street, its passenger thankfully no longer able to cause harm. As Cathy stood there, she became aware of a presence beside them. He was in her peripheral vision for some time before she spoke.

'Well?' she asked. 'What do you have to say about it all then?'

The man, who was commonly known about the town as Carbolic, was as brazen as anyone might have imagined.

'Always hated that one; Carol,' he said. 'If you'd just asked, I'd have told you it was her. Not all-there,' he said and tapped his forehead.

With that, he sloped off down the street.

'One person's madness affected so many others' lives,' Holly said.

Cathy looked at the young, fragile woman and nodded.

## 36

'But I still don't understand,' Marie said, shaking her head with what seemed to be a genuine annoyance.

They were sitting together on ward thirty-two by Thomas's bed. He had surprised everyone, including his orthopaedic surgeons, by announcing that morning that he wanted to get up and have a news with folk about the place. It seemed that he had been pushed in a wheelchair to the tv room and had sat for a good hour regaling his new acquaintances with tales of murder and mayhem. His nurses were apparently, quite taken with him and he adopted his new role as ward mascot with great delight.

Cathy had called earlier to say that she had spoken to the police that morning. It seemed that Carol had now made a full confession. The detective said that he thought with the help of a clever lawyer, she might plead insanity, but apparently, he was having none of it.

Holly looked across the room at Thomas, who was now sitting up in bed after his adventures and looking pleased with himself. She had spoken with one of the surgeons who confirmed that his injuries would not trouble him in the future. He should return to as independent a life as he wished for, once he had healed. Thomas grinned at her and mouthed 'told you,' for about the millionth time that day.

'I know. I'm not the best at explaining things,' Holly said, returning to Marie.

'So, you're saying that Carol, as a social worker at the time, had become mentally ill, and had been admitted to Fernibanks?'

'I'm afraid so. I think she found the job very hard. She was friendly with Tricia on the ward even back then. Tricia was a student nurse at the time.'

'So brutal though,' Marie said.

Holly agreed. 'Yes. Both Carol's rough justice for the psychiatrist and then, for Betty herself when she said she needed to speak out and clear her conscience.'

'She was a horrible woman.'

'Who, Carol?' Holly asked.

'No Betty.' Marie said quite severely. 'She didn't deserve to die that way, and she probably lived a dreadful life herself after she gave up the hospital, but she was a horrible woman all the same.'

'The saddest thing is that she was dying anyway. I had suspected it for a while myself. Her weight loss ... When I heard she had a hospital appointment that afternoon, I assumed that it must be the case. Breast cancer,' Holly explained.

'How sad,' Marie said. She glanced across at Thomas again. 'But she was a nasty piece of work all the same.' She shook her head. 'Not fit to be a mother at all,' Marie looked at the young girl, perhaps to check that her words had landed.

'You knew?' Holly asked, surprised. 'I thought I had been the clever one, all along.'

Marie smiled and the corners of her eyes glistened. 'It's

funny,' she said. 'For a while, I thought you had killed Betty for that reason. That was until I saw how you had become with Thomas. Then I couldn't have suspected you for a minute.'

'They told me that I was found in a doorway up at the old hospital,' Holly said. 'Discarded like a piece of tat, with only a blanket and a binbag to keep me warm. You'd have thought as a nurse, she might have done a bit better for me. I suppose Betty must have been near enough menopausal herself when she had me. I wonder if my father really was the dreadful psychiatrist. Had he forced himself on Betty? Was I the dreadful result? I think I'd rather not know. Betty must have struggled to conceal the pregnancy from her staff. I don't know how she managed. I only found out I was adopted by chance, and that was barely months ago. I knew Fernibanks was part of it. It was all I came to this town armed with. Just a name and a story.' Holly knew that she sounded bitter. 'How did you work it out anyway?' she asked.

'I think the eyes,' Marie said slowly. 'Yes, probably that, and strangely, you had some of her mannerisms, which is surprising given that you were never brought up by her.'

'I'm a monster like her, and worst,' Holly said savagely. 'I can't help myself sometimes. I've no empathy at all.'

'You're not a monster,' the old woman said sadly. 'And as for the empathy, well I've seen how you are with Thomas. You will make a wonderful doctor in the future, I'm sure. You're just a bit lost. You're an adult whose child-self hasn't healed. There are a few of those about,' she glanced across once more at the man who had captured her own heart. 'You just need to find someone who will love you like that awful woman should have done. Your adoptive mother I presume ...?'

'Oh, I've messed up big time there,' Holly said.

'Perhaps it's time to face up to a few things instead of

running, or drowning your sorrows,' the old woman said, smiling a little. 'Time to go home and make amends. The people who love you are your real family after all. You've found your vocation, now allow everything else to fall into place.'

## 37

'I don't know what to say,' Cathy admitted. Her face was flushed, but she met his gaze all the same. She had pinned the charity ribbon Carol had given her, to the neck of her blouse. She flicked the material absently, and catching herself, she smiled.

It was a week later and Cathy for one was glad that the whole business was cleared up. Betty Scott had plagued her thoughts now for so long that she felt she had been going half-mad.

Alex shifted beside her and took a sip of his wine. 'Glainkirk will never be quite the same,' he said. 'It's the end of an era. With both Carol and Betty gone, the charity bosses have asked if any of the rest of the volunteers are willing to step up to the mark, and take on the running of the shop.'

'And?' Cathy asked. 'Tricia, maybe? Or you?'

'I think I've done my time,' he smiled. 'Fresh start for me. Time to move on.'

Cathy looked at him in surprise.

'Move on, but not away,' he said in answer. 'The bank's come through finally. I've been given the loan I was after and I'm setting up my own business. Although, after our recent breaking and entering, I think it's a little hypocritical.' He laughed, and then to her look of confusion, he explained: 'Security. I'm starting up a security advisory business. What with my experience in the police, it seems natural, you know?'

Cathy grinned. She couldn't help herself. 'I can't believe I thought it was you; the murderer, I mean. I really did,' she said. 'For a while there, I imagined I had made the most dreadful mistake having anything to do with you, Alex. I wished our paths had never crossed when I found you in that horrible charity shop.'

He placed his wine glass on the table and turned to her.

'And now?' he asked.

But Cathy didn't need to answer.

# ACKNOWLEDGMENTS

To my editor Amanda, a massive thank you. Seriously, without your expertise, this book wouldn't be half of what it is now. Many thanks to my father for his critical eye over the final days, but also for his encouragement throughout - that goes for my mother also. Your championship and love has been so appreciated. As always, thank you to my beloved husband, who hates all the lovey-dovey stuff, but really does steady the ship when I'm on a manic writing spree!

Finally, thank you to all of the people who told me that they enjoyed *Murder and Malpractice* enough to want the series to continue. I can't wait to share book three with you very soon!

## THANK YOU!

I do hope that you have enjoyed reading book two in the Dr Cathy Moreland Mystery series. If you'd like to hear about future releases and offers, please visit my website http://mairichong.com and sign up to my mailing list. I'd love to have you on board. I'm also often active on Facebook (Mairi Chong Author) and twitter @mairichong. Do pop by and say hello!

Finally, if you have enjoyed the book, please consider recommending it to a friend or writing a review. It would mean the world to me.

Printed in Great Britain
by Amazon